1994

THE LORD OF MISRULE

By Paul Halter

The Lord of Misrule

First published in French in 1994 by
Editions du Masque – Hachette Livre as *Le Roi du Desordre*

For information, contact: pugmire1@yahoo.com

FIRST AMERICAN EDITION
Library of Congress Cataloging-in-Publication Data
Halter, Paul
[*Le Roi du Desordre*. English]
The Lord of Misrule / Paul Halter;
translated from the French by John Pugmire

1

THE TINKLING OF TINY BELLS

"Life is full of coincidences. Now there's a remarkable enough phrase to begin our story."

It was with these words that Owen Burns' play *The Importance of Being Archie Bow* began; the play which had made all London cry – with laughter or anger? – several years ago, and which had caused much ink to flow, that having indubitably been the primary objective of its author. If I quote Owen here, it is not only because it gives an insight – to any reader still unaware of it – of his philosophy, but also because the first statement describes perfectly the extraordinary sequence of events I was privileged to witness some time ago and which I shall now describe.

After some hesitation, I have opted to present the facts, not as they occurred chronologically, but in the order in which they appeared to me. The reader will thus be in the position to appreciate more readily the perplexity, the anguish, and the fear – even terror – that I, as a young man in his mid-twenties (the same age as Owen), experienced.

As I said before, life is full of coincidences, the manner in which Owen and I met being a perfect illustration. The encounter, although occurring a year before the principal events, remains important because it was immediately followed by another which not only confirmed the celebrated phrase, but turned out to have been the true starting point of the sombre tragedy.

It was on an afternoon just before Christmas at the turn of the last century – that is to say, the late 1890s – that I saw Owen Burns for the first time. Through the great thoroughfares of London, a joyful crowd squelched its way dexterously in the slush to admire the magnificent decorations on display in the multitude of store windows. Every kind of merchandise was festooned with holly and silvered garlands to attract the covetous gaze of the passers-by. As for myself, I watched the natives with as much interest as I watched the commercial extravaganza and marvelled at their simple contentment, certainly greater than mine.

Two weeks earlier, I had landed in Portsmouth, after having left my native South Africa where my parents had been killed a year earlier in a tragic rail accident in Cape Province where my father had been a high-ranking government official. He had managed his private investments with the same flair he had shown in his professional life, with the result that I was able to face the future without financial concern. Why had I chosen to leave for England? To put behind me the tragedy which had turned my life upside-down? That was certainly one reason, but not the only one.

For some time, I had felt a vague but indefinable artistic yearning growing in me. I wandered aimlessly between literature, music, architecture, and drawing. The only thing I was sure about was that I needed to discover my "voice," which I almost certainly wouldn't be able to do in South Africa, but in cities like London, Paris, or Rome. And that's how, ten days after I landed, I found myself wandering the streets of London, asking myself about my future, and in search of that mysterious "voice." I had no idea that I was about to find it, in the person of someone who cultivated art for art's sake, and who would become my friend.

How to describe Owen Burns? I shall always see him as he was that day, standing in front of the florist, holding a fragile rosebud in his pudgy fingers. Tall and rather corpulent, with sensuous lips and sleepy eyes, he exuded a majestic simplicity pleasantly devoid of any affectation. The lazy expression in his eyes could not completely conceal the glint of a lively intelligence lurking there. The orange-coloured woollen suit he was wearing was exceedingly difficult to ignore, as was the artificial blue carnation in his buttonhole.

'This one?' asked the girl, looking quizzically at the flower Owen was holding. 'I'm not trying to influence your choice, sir, but if you're only going to pick one flower, may I suggest another one. They're all the same price and, frankly, this one –.'

'I didn't say I'd take this: I said I'd take these,' replied Owen, pronouncing each syllable carefully. 'The one I have in my hand is the only one I won't take.'

The girl stood dumbfounded for a moment, and then stammered:
'I don't understand, sir.'

'This flower,' he repeated, waving it under the poor girl's nose, 'is the one I'm not taking.'

'I – I still don't understand.'

Owen Burns looked slowly all around him on the street, before his gaze lighted on me.

'I am, nevertheless, speaking the King's English, don't you agree, my dear sir? And what I'm saying seems abundantly clear: the flower I'm holding in my hand is the one I shan't take. Therefore it follows that I shall take all the others, *all the others*.'

The little florist's eyes opened wide in astonishment as she surveyed her entire merchandise. Meanwhile, as Owen continued to look questioningly at me, I replied without thinking:

'Yes, of course. It's clear, quite clear. You'll buy everything but that one.'

I was just as intrigued as all the passers-by who, having heard the conversation, had gathered around the kiosk, for it was clear that Burns would find it almost impossible to take all the flowers away with him. But the surprises had just started.

In a majestically off-handed manner, Owen tossed a bundle of pound notes at the awestruck girl and said, casually:

'That should cover it, I think. I'd be very obliged if you would have them delivered to Miss Jane Baker, at the Beltram Hotel, on behalf of Owen Burns.'

Still unable to utter a sound, the florist merely nodded. Her customer turned to me and observed:

'These roses are quite magnificent, aren't they? I had to cover the whole of London to find such quality at this time of year.'

'They're greenhouse grown, sir,' declared the girl proudly, as she hastened to gather the flowers into a sumptuous bouquet.

Whereupon the rose-lover beckoned to an approaching hackney cab and, once the driver had pulled up, announced in a loud voice:

'"Gray's," in Regent Street. And hurry!'

For a few seconds, the cabbie's face registered the same reaction as the florist's and, for that matter, the faces of the increasing number of bystanders who had stopped to witness the ever more curious actions of the equally curious Owen Burns.

The cabbie glanced over his shoulder at the opposite side of the street where, over the windows of a large store, could be seen, in vermillion letters on a dark yellow background, the word "Gray's."

He looked back at his potential customer and asked, with a frown:

'"Gray's," Regent Street? Is that what you said?'

'Yes, I believe so.'

The cabbie pointed a thumb at the store across the street.

'Don't you know it's right opposite?'

'Why all these questions?' exclaimed Burns. 'Of course I know. I'm not in the habit of asking to be taken to places I don't know.'

'But if you're in such a hurry –.'

'That's what I said, isn't it? So now tell me if you're going to take me or not. There's not a moment to lose!'

The cabbie raised his eyes to the heavens. Once his fare had settled disdainfully in his seat, he cracked his whip and they were on their way. I was not the only one to watch in disbelief as the cab, reaching the nearest street corner, executed a u-turn to end up in front of the store immediately opposite the spot it had just left. Seeing Burns get out and enter the store, I assumed I had seen the end of the strange business. But I was quite wrong as, less than a minute after he had entered the store, an employee appeared at the door calling for a doctor at the top of his voice: a gentleman customer had been taken ill. A number of us pushed our way to the storefront, and I was only slightly surprised to find that it was Owen Burns who had fainted and was now lying on the floor in the middle of the salesroom. I was, however, considerably more surprised when, having recovered consciousness, he announced to all and sundry: 'My God, how dreadful! What an abominably ill-assorted collection. It's more than I can bear to look at. Please take me out of here immediately!'

I must make it clear that the furniture at Gray's, while not being a model of refinement, was perfectly presentable. So what was Owen Burns playing at? Was his artistic sensitivity so heightened that he fainted at the slightest lack of harmony? I listened to the comments of the crowd around me: 'Those Oxford types are always trying to draw attention to themselves.' 'A poet, did you say? More like a madman.' 'It's the same thing, isn't it?' 'That's him! That's the chap we saw the other day, walking down Piccadilly contemplating a flower.' 'And almost caused an accident by trying to retrieve a bunch of flowers in front of an oncoming bus.' 'I'm not surprised he's fallen for that American actress Jane Baker. She's just like him: no education.' 'He's a loony, that one.' 'What's the world coming to?'

I had more or less forgotten about Owen Burns when, later that afternoon, I left the tea-room replenished but still intent on discovering more of the city. I decided to leave the well-to-do areas in search of more humble surroundings.

Gradually the houses became smaller and brick construction replaced stone. The red of the bricks became duller and dirtier as well, yet at the same time the spirit of Christmas seemed to become warmer, and perhaps simpler and more natural; more natural than in the more respectable areas, for here there were children playing in the streets, gleefully sipping and sliding on the ice. Night was falling and the gas-lamps had just been lit, their scintillating light throwing a golden halo around the window displays in the modest shops. The leaves of the holly wreaths gleamed in reflection and the pyramids of oranges seemed aglow. Even though I had partaken of several scones with my tea, I was unable to resist a succulent apple turnover from one of the pastry shops. The painted dolls and the wooden horses in the toyshops were roughly finished, but the eyes of the children pressing their noses against the glass shone with an excitement I hadn't seen elsewhere that afternoon.

Nonetheless, nothing could compare to the fascination on the face of a young boy, almost a child, whom I noticed a little farther on, standing in front of a poultry shop. The proprietor had just started to take down the merchandise from the window where it had been hanging. The youngster wasn't exactly in rags, but the condition of the old black hat that kept falling over his eyes spoke volumes about his condition. He was ogling a goose: a goose so large it was doubtful he could even carry it. An expression of bitterness crossed his face when I enquired the price, but it changed to astonished delight when I paid for it and placed it in his arms, wishing him a Merry Christmas the while. Obviously fearful I might change my mind, he turned quickly to leave. But before going he offered me his oversize hat and I instinctively realised it would be a mistake on my part to refuse such a gift.

I continued on my walk, congratulating myself on my generosity, but unable nevertheless to suppress the feeling that I had acted more for the pleasure of seeing the youngster's surprised reaction than out of any deep-seated purity of the soul. In vain I searched my conscience, as I continued to penetrate farther and farther into the impoverished neighbourhood where the very walls oozed poverty. The sparkling whiteness of the snow which covered roofs, sheds, window frames and every projecting surface contrasted cruelly with the leprous walls of the dingy rows of houses, made even more sinister by the encroaching darkness. The streets were nevertheless animated and the shouts, the conversations and the laughter, although uncouth and shrill, were no less warm for all that. I wistfully recalled my own youth and, feeling somewhat emotional, I moved to get a closer look at an old man endlessly turning the handle of his barrel organ. Despite his top-hat, which had seen better days, he had a certain bearing and a dignity which was apparent in his clear gaze. Curiously, the same demeanour could be seen in his companion: a small monkey perched on top of the organ, from which vantage point he stared wild-eyed at the passers-by from under a lopsided cocked-hat, of which he seemed inordinately proud.

Weary yet fascinated, I remained there watching the crowd of rosy-cheeked individuals milling around the organ player and listening to their hoary old favourites, when, suddenly, I heard a voice which seemed vaguely familiar murmuring in my ear:

'You seem to be enjoying the touching spectacle as much as I…'

I turned round and immediately recognised the fellow whose strange behaviour had intrigued so many earlier that day. Owen Burns had exchanged his orange suit for a more sporting ensemble of checked jacket and peaked cap which, despite being more classical in style, nevertheless attracted attention.

'A remarkable sight,' I stammered, surprised and disconcerted by his sudden appearance. 'Though perhaps not exactly –.'

'It was indeed you I met this afternoon in front of the florist's, was it not? I never forget a face.'

I acknowledged as much and introduced myself, adding with a startling lack of originality:

'Life is full of coincidences.'

He stared hard at me and replied:

'That's very profound. You must be an artist, if I'm not mistaken?'

I was quite taken aback.

'Well…that is to say… But how…?'

'The master knows how to recognise a disciple. There's more feeling and more poetry here than anywhere else in the city, don't you think? That's what was in your mind, wasn't it?'

After that somewhat unceremonious introduction, Owen Burns let me lead the conversation and I surprised myself how quickly I confided my thoughts in him, confirming his premise. As I talked, I noticed how attentively he was listening, and his exclamations and air of understanding encouraged me to continue. He was obviously eccentric, but sympathetic and with a lively mind. Having him as a friend would surely be the perfect antidote to any depression I might feel during my stay in London. That thought had just crossed my mind when I once again had cause to wonder about his mental equilibrium as he declared:

'I don't, of course, know what you believe to be your artistic calling, but in a way you've just found it, for Art is standing before you at this very moment. Heavens above! I've just remembered a most beautiful American is waiting to have dinner with me. I shall be late!'

As he took his departure he pressed his visiting card into my hand, saying:

'Come and see me whenever you wish, so we may continue this most fulfilling conversation.'

I stood there for some time, looking at the street corner around which he had vanished at high speed, thinking about my initial impression of him and unable to persuade myself to revise it. Then, as the snow began to fall again, I decided it was time to leave. Donning the old hat the urchin had given me, I convinced myself I was less likely that way to attract attention than was Owen Burns. As I reached a side-street, a snowball hit me full in the face, and I saw two young brats running away as fast as they could go. The idea of pursuing them was farthest from my mind; I felt more like smiling, for it had crowned a day full of buffoonery. I hadn't even made a move to wipe the snow off my face when I saw *her*...

A merchant's cart pulled by a pony bedecked with ribbons and tiny tinkling bells had just passed me. I was standing under a gas lamp not far from the intersection, so that when *she* came round the corner she appeared under a cone of light. I had never seen such a lovely face: bright red lips and a pearly white, almost transparent, complexion, framed by jet-black curls. She was slender and graceful and absolutely adorable, wearing a little hat decorated with a flower as delicate and fragile as herself. Three or four seconds went by as we stood still, looking silently at each other, before an expression of terror crossed her face. She let out a heartrending shriek and started to run back whence she had come.

It was hardly credible. Was it I who had frightened her to that point? I couldn't and wouldn't believe it. I ran after her and only caught up with her with great difficulty, for she seemed truly afraid of me. I'd lost my hat during the chase, but that was of little importance; I was holding the adorable little bird in my arms and trying to reassure her:

'For Heaven's sake, calm down. I mean you no harm.'

She shivered again, but her anxiety had receded and my presence seemed to comfort her. Nevertheless, her pronouncement was very strange:

'The white mask...the tinkling of tiny bells...I thought it was him...'

I couldn't quite follow what she said after that, but I thought I heard the words "Lord" and "Misrule."

'Please, I beg of you, if you're in any kind of danger, please tell me.'

For a moment, as we looked at each other, the distress in her eyes overwhelmed me.

'Help me,' she murmured.

But she pulled herself together immediately and, in a clear, firm voice declared:

'Forgive me. I've been behaving like an idiot.'

She muttered a few polite phrases and left quickly. For a moment I thought about following her, but her abrupt change in tone and the determined manner of her departure dissuaded me. It seemed obvious to me that some terrible secret weighed heavily on her young shoulders. I thought of all sorts of possibilities, without ever imagining for a second that I would see her again the following year and witness with her the most extraordinary of murders.

2

WHERE I AM CHARGED WITH A STRANGE MISSION

From the time of his youth, my paternal grandfather Achilles Stock had been a strapping fellow with a square jaw and thick golden locks, bursting with robust health and limitless energy. A multitude of ideas teemed in his fertile imagination but, alas! his indecisiveness prevented him from ever making his fortune, and he died in the Scottish city where he was born: Edinburgh. The only project he ever managed successfully, so to speak, was the education and upbringing of my father.

Gentle reader, rest assured I shall not bore you further with my family history. I mentioned my grandfather only to avoid describing myself in detail, for it has been said that I bear a close resemblance to him both physically and morally; in addition to which I have the same first name. And it was in his birthplace that I spent much of the time that followed the events related in the preceding chapter. A friend – not Owen Burns, but through whom I had made acquaintance – had managed to persuade me to help him promote an Edinburgh artist. With my friend's enthusiasm and my financial resources we sponsored a number of exhibitions there which met with unqualified but fleeting success, to the point that I only barely recovered my outlay. This episode in my life actually has nothing whatsoever to do with the story, but did take me hither and thither in the realm and consequently away from London and Owen. It was just before the following Christmas, therefore, that I returned to the capital.

Having only met a few times before my departure, Owen and I were not yet on intimate terms. But he nevertheless evinced great pleasure on seeing me again when I called on him at his flat near St. James's Square to announce my return. Before describing that encounter, whose consequences would result in this story being written, I need to make some observations about Owen's public *persona*, which was a constant source of amazement to even his closest friends, and to the promotion of which he devoted much talent and ingenuity. Within the space of a few months, he had managed to gain a notoriety even outside the capital itself. I had picked up snippets about his exploits from the Scottish press, and it was already clear to me that those in which I had already participated were just the beginnings. He declared himself to be aesthete, thinker, philosopher, poet, writer – and who knows what else – whose sole preoccupation was the art of Art, which he cultivated to the point of absurdity on occasion. The aphorisms and swift rejoinders which he tossed off so negligently amused or shocked, but always surprised. His wit had captivated the upper classes and his presence was in high demand at salons and soirees. In the course of a private evening attended by Scotland Yard's higher ranks, he once declared that "vulgarity was a crime but crime, on the other hand, was never vulgar." An assertion which, it hardly goes without saying, did not go down well. He had gone on to say that a seemingly impossible crime could, if it were extraordinary enough in nature, attain the level of art – and the perpetrator therefore a sort of artist – adding that he made it a point of solving every apparently inexplicable crime because, as an artist himself, he could readily appreciate the efforts of a kindred spirit. He had been put to the test once or twice with, it seems, some success – although the celebrated London police could hardly have been expected to broadcast the fact. Frankly, his success did not surprise me, for I had already observed that Owen had been blessed with a quite extraordinary perspicacity.

So, as I was saying, Owen welcomed me warmly that evening. I was deeply moved at the time, as I had not yet learned what he had in the back of his mind. He was wearing a deep blue satin dressing gown embroidered with golden arabesques.

'My dear Achilles,' he declared, after having helped me out of my raincoat and bowler hat. 'You can't imagine how happy I am to see you. Come over here and sit down. We can savour the delights of idleness, which is the mother of genius, in case you didn't know. Would you care to join me in a small whisky?'

'It's a little early, I fear –.'

'Come, come. I know you can resist many things, but never temptation.'

While Owen was serving me I looked around the room which, contrary to what I might have expected from someone who was the epitome of instability, had scarcely changed. A detailed description would take up too much space, given the abundance of every kind of object. Nevertheless I must mention his precious statues of china porcelain for, if one day he should ever read this book, he would never forgive me if I neglected to do so.

He returned with the drinks, offered me a cigar, lit one himself, then settled down in an armchair opposite mine.

'Now, Achilles, tell me what you've been up to all these months. Did you ever find your calling: that mysterious discipline whose power you could sense even though you couldn't quite describe it?'

I told him about the art exhibitions and my narrow escape from ruin. He listened without interrupting me; then, as I spoke of his friend my ex-associate, he interrupted disdainfully:

'Oscar is an idiot who only talks sense at breakfast. It's not your fault. I should have warned you that you were running a great risk with that philistine.' He refilled my glass. 'If you only knew, Achilles, how happy I am to see you again. I was becoming really bored in this dismal place with its stultified citizens, plunged in a sort of intellectual solitude; the only comfort being my certitude of their immense inferiority. But keep on with your story, it's far more interesting.'

As I continued my story, detailing my failures, I was surprised by the cordial warmth and passionate interest on the part of my host, which seemed a little excessive given the infrequency and brevity of our previous encounters.

'How I envy you,' he said, nodding his head sympathetically as I concluded my tale. 'You've acquired considerable experience of life. You've strengthened your character while at the same time enriching your spirit. You certainly haven't wasted your time.' He was speaking very earnestly while observing a curl of smoke as it rose to the ceiling. 'You know, Achilles, I've always thought you as a wild animal in need of wide horizons. You have an innate yearning for adventure and taking risks.'

'There's some truth to that,' I replied naively, 'You see, in South Africa –.'

'You were in South Africa? But of course, I'd forgotten, you'd already told me. Excellent, excellent!'

'I beg your pardon?'

'Nothing, nothing. So you like danger, mystery with a dash of the exotic…'

What was he trying to say? I was still asking myself the question when he continued in a more measured tone:

'You don't have anything urgent on just now, do you? May I take it you're more or less free at the moment? Free to commit yourself body and soul to Art?'

I noticed that he avoided looking at me as he pulled on his cigar, apparently lost in thought. I waited expectantly. Suddenly he sprang to his feet, as if propelled by a spring:

'Achilles, I have a proposition to make. I suggest you take a few days off, say two weeks, during which you will be able to increase your powers of observation and, as a consequence, your perception of art. Furthermore, your stay will be seasoned with a dash of danger

13

and a pinch of mystery – in other words, everything you could possibly wish for. What do you say?'

I was naturally intrigued, but waited a decent interval before asking for more detail. Pacing to and fro in the room, head down, Owen spoke rapidly:

'I'm not sure you're aware of this, but I have been known to give the police a hand when they find themselves at a dead end. It all began as the result of a stupid bet, but that's of no consequence. You know how these things happen. I've put my artistic faculties at their service from time to time and this or that official has sought me out to beg me for help. Trifling stuff usually: theft of family jewels, that sort of thing. But the other day....'

He paused for effect in front of one of his beloved porcelain statuettes and stroked it pensively with a single finger before continuing in a more decisive tone:

'What I'm about to ask of you is rather delicate, because it's truly an extraordinary business. One which will require an exceptional acuity of the senses.'

'I don't understand. If you're the one who plays detective in his spare time, I don't see –.'

'Quite,' he cut in. 'It just so happens that I'm currently very busy...Oh, why try and invent a story!' He came over to sit beside me. 'Achilles, do you know what it is to love? To love as much as I love beauty? *She* is leaving for the continent in five days and nothing in the world must be allowed to prevent me spending the last few precious moments with her!' He spoke with a passion and an intensity which I found convincing. 'Achilles, if you could see her...she's so beautiful .'

'I see.'

'Ah! You see her?'

'Her, no. But I see what you're asking of me. You want me to take your place.'

'Achilles, you're doing me an enormous favour.'

'I haven't agreed yet. But while I'm thinking it over, give me some more details.'

Head down, he started pacing the room once again in silence.

'As I was saying,' he said eventually, 'it's a very unusual business which demands careful handling. What I would prefer is for you to go there without any preconceived ideas, soak up the atmosphere, and dispassionately take note of the smallest gesture and slightest movement of everyone involved. Fill your head with information so clear and so precise that I could have been there myself; in essence, be my eyes and ears. Do you get my drift?'

'Only too well,' I replied brusquely.

'After you've been there a few days, we can meet secretly and compare notes. At that point, I may be able to explain the problem in more detail.'

'If I understand correctly, I am to appear in an unfamiliar place amongst people unknown to me?'

Thereupon, Owen gave me a very rough description of the destination and the main protagonists. A certain Charles Mansfield lived in a vast residence situated on the outskirts of a small village just outside London. He had two daughters: Daphne and Sibyl. The latter, the older of the two, was due to marry a rich merchant, one Samuel Piggott, a friend of her father. Piggott had a sister, Catherine, and a business associate, Edgar Forbes; all three were in the habit of spending Christmas at the Mansfield's.

I enquired whether I should present myself as a detective, whereupon he threw his arms in the air and replied:

'Absolutely not! Ah, there's something I forgot to tell you....'

His face clouded again and he explained he had worked out a strategy with his client which would allow me to be present without attracting suspicion. He – that is, I – would be the fiancé.

'Well, I must confess it's beginning to sound more interesting. Which of the daughters is your client?'

'Actually, neither. You're engaged to Piggott's sister, who's worried about her brother.' He looked at me and there was a catch in his voice. 'She's going on forty, and isn't exactly a beauty, although that's of no importance.'

'Is she ugly?'

He cleared his throat:

'That's a harsh word. Think of it this way: you'll gain a lot of credibility if you're seen in the company of someone who – let us say – has not been over-blessed by nature.'

Who in his right mind would have accepted such a mission? Frankly, I didn't know anyone. I didn't know anyone, that is, who would have let Owen wrap him round his little finger as he did me that evening, using every trick in the book to persuade me. In the end, it was the lure of the mystery which proved decisive.

When we were done, he glanced at the clock and leapt to his feet.

'Heavens above, she'll be here at any moment. Achilles, you must leave right away.'

'Who's coming, the charming Miss Piggott?' I asked through clenched teeth.

'No – Ah! I see you've recovered your sense of humour. And now, hurry along. I'll get word to you tomorrow. Be ready to leave by late afternoon.'

He accompanied me to the door, his arm around my shoulder in a friendly manner. Even though the winter that year was particularly harsh, it wasn't the cold that was making me shiver.

'Oh, there's one other thing I forgot to mention,' he said as I was just about to leave. 'While you're down there, if you happen to see a ghastly white face like a sort of mask one night, or if you hear tiny bells tinkling, you need to be a bit careful. *You might be in mortal peril.*'

3

SILHOUETTE IN THE SNOW

The next day, the snow fell without interruption. It stopped around tea-time and the capital was plunged into a sudden and intense cold. It was at just about that time that I found myself standing, stamping my feet, at the south east corner of Russell Square, where Owen's message had told me a messenger would come to find me.

I called it a message, not a letter, for it consisted of a few lines scribbled on a piece of paper which had been handed to me two hours earlier. A text of an insolent brevity, in view of subsequent events. It told me almost nothing beyond what had been said the night before, except in the matter of Miss Catherine Piggott and our professed relationship. The tone was ironic: "Regarding your fiancée, my dear Achilles, please don't trouble yourself: I dropped her a line last night to explain the slight change in plans. I'm quite sure that, at this very moment, having received my message, the fair lady cannot contain her impatience to meet you. No doubt you will be pampered and fussed over throughout your stay, but you must nevertheless remember to keep your eyes open. I shall contact you in two or three days." I could have strangled him.

The clock of the nearby church had just struck five when a vehicle drew alongside. It was a sort of family omnibus, its roof packed with thick bundles and miscellaneous packages. After he had brought his whinnying carriage to rest, I explained to the coachman that I was a friend of Miss Piggott, and he beckoned me to climb in. At first, all I could see of him was a greatcoat and a hat pulled down over his eyes, but I was able to make his acquaintance shortly thereafter when we stopped in front of a shop to make some purchases. Nicholas Dudley was a strapping fellow of some forty years and, despite a gruff manner, it took only a few minutes for me to take a liking to him.

'What weather, sir,' he said, rubbing his hands together. 'We haven't seen such cold for years. Mary told me we'd be having problems with the water if'n it continues.'

Mary, he explained to me, was his wife, a charming little woman with many fine qualities, for whom he thanked the Lord every day for sending his way. They both worked for the Mansfields, and lived with them. Mary was head cook and virtually ran the house, while he took care of the horses and the transportation, for which he also had other customers in the village. He usually travelled up to town once a day but, with the approaching holidays, he found himself frequently going twice. He spoke to me, too, about the good Mr. Piggott and his charming and refined sister, on whom he dwelled at some length in a clumsy attempt to extract information from me.

'I imagine you haven't known her very long?' he asked cheerfully, adjusting his headgear.

'That's right,' I replied nonchalantly.

He leaned closer and spoke in a confidential whisper:

'You know, there's quite an age difference between Mary and myself -- in the opposite sense -- but that doesn't matter if you get along well with each other.'

I nodded in agreement, cursing Owen under my breath for having put me in such a position. I was beginning to wonder what Miss Catherine Piggott must look like for Nicholas to be making such an observation. Encouraged by my silence, he continued:

'Besides, it's the same for Mr. Piggott and Miss Sibyl, you know. Mind you, they've known each other for quite some time. They'd be married now, but for... Well, you must know what I'm talking about.'

I confessed my ignorance.

'Well, if you haven't known each other for very long, it's understandable. As I was saying, they'd be already married but for the tragedy and all what happened after, like.'

'Tragedy? What tragedy?'

'Why, Edwin's death, that's what. Edwin, Sibyl's brother. He was about your age, as well. It gave her a right shock at the time. That was three years ago.'

'Was it an accident?'

'An accident?' Nicholas echoed, a startled expression on his face. 'Not really. He was killed. Murdered.'

'Murdered, for heaven's sake! I hope they caught the villain.'

The coachman looked askance it me.

'You mean nobody's told you about it? Don't you know that HE returns at Christmastime every year? Before poor Edwin there was old George. And last year it was Jim's turn. He was the butcher, a lively sort of bloke who wouldn't have hurt a fly.' He opened the carriage door. 'We'd best be on our way, if we're to be there in time for supper.'

I climbed in, my head in a whirl. I scarcely noticed the forward jolt that followed the crack of the driver's whip. As the carriage sped along the snow-covered road, I tried to make sense of the situation with the few facts at my disposal. For I had no intention of simply being dear Owen's "eyes and ears." Nothing and no-one was going to stop me thinking…

…A maiden lady by the name of Catherine Piggott had sought out my friend for help because she was worried about her brother Samuel, who was due to marry Sibyl, whose brother had been murdered three years earlier by a mysterious individual known as "HE", who had apparently had other victims before that. It's difficult – if not impossible – not to have preconceived ideas about those involved and I must confess to having formed an extremely negative opinion about the rich merchant who was about to marry his best friend's daughter, and an equally prejudiced opinion about his sister. Following the same line of thought, I felt a decided lack of sympathy for Charles Mansfield for having agreed to give his daughter's hand in marriage to someone who could be her father. As of now, only Daphne and Forbes, Piggott's partner, had failed to incur my premature displeasure.

It seemed to me that Miss Piggott's concern for her brother was in all likelihood prompted by the tragedies which seemed to occur every Christmas. It wasn't too far-fetched to conclude that Piggott's life was in danger. As to the nature of the menace, I had very few clues other than the warning my friend had passed on to me regarding white faces and little tinkling bells, all of which seemed rather too vague.

I was lost in thought, ruminating on all the above, when in my mind's eye I suddenly saw the image of the young woman I had met in the squalid streets of London, who had taken flight almost immediately afterwards. She, too, had spoken of a white mask and the tinkling of tiny bells.

It was probably at that point that I became truly aware of the danger which awaited me. The phrases "white mask" and "tinkling bells" had no significance in themselves, yet one sensed an underlying menace: invisible, yet all the more disturbing for that. The investigation now appeared to me in a completely different light: no longer the exercise in pure observation and deduction that Owen had described in order to lure me down there. No, that wasn't fair; after all, he had warned me that it was a serious matter and potentially full of risk.

Night had already fallen by the time we reached the outskirts of the city. The noise and turmoil of the capital were behind us and there were fewer carriages and well-lit areas. The muffled sound of the horses' hooves on the snow was accompanied by the irritating squeaking of the wheels. Soon, there was nothing but a scattering of isolated houses in the great expanse of whiteness.

If I have been somewhat vague about the dates so far, it's not altogether by accident. Nor is it by chance that I have waited so long to recount what happened and taken the precaution of changing the names of the protagonists. For even today I believe there are still many who would find the memory of the terrible events painful in the extreme. My interest lies solely in narrating the elements which made this such a bewildering mystery. Consequently, I shall be equally vague about the name and location of the small village which we traversed after an hour of travel, and which consisted merely of a few humble houses, a bridge, a river and a church, lost in the middle of snow-covered fields swept by a glacial wind. To the north, at the edge of the village, the terrain was more hilly and it was in this direction that we headed.

Less than a minute later, Nicholas Dudley's booming voice announced our imminent arrival. It was a clear night and, by the light from the stars and the waxing moon, I was able to discern a vast two-story Tudor residence standing in total isolation. Two wings were visible, each as long as the central building to which they were attached and each with a tower; a wooden gallery, from which jousts and hunts were doubtless once observed, connected the two towers.

A shout from the driver drew my attention elsewhere and I observed a figure which appeared to be moving away from the residence. Upon spotting us it stopped, hanging slightly back from the road. As soon as Nicholas had drawn to a halt, I got down from the carriage to ask him what was happening.

With one hand on the reins, Nicholas stood stock still staring at the figure, a dark silhouette in a vast expanse of white, while the breath from the horse's nostrils formed clouds of steam in the frigid air. After some hesitation, the figure started towards us. As it approached, I could see it was a fellow only slightly younger than I and simply dressed. He seemed out of sorts and kept his head down, avoiding my gaze, as we watched him walk dispiritedly towards the village. Nicholas, having climbed back into his seat, growled:

'Well, that's someone we haven't seen for quite a while.'

'Who was it?'

'Harry Nichols. He was once one of Sibyl's admirers. I wonder what he's doing around here now? He looked as though he had something on his conscience. I wonder if...'

'He certainly didn't look as though he'd be easy to deal with,' I observed, noting the expression of Nicholas's face, which seemed to be registering great relief after a rude shock. 'But tell me: why did you stop the carriage?'

'Because –,' he stammered, 'because I mistook him for – for someone else.'

Someone else.

He didn't elaborate and I climbed back into my seat, not, I must admit, very reassured by his last words. My stomach was tied in knots as we pulled up in front of the main door, but for another reason: how was I going to play my role as fiancé?

Then something happened which seemed to be amusing and very convenient at the time, but which quickly turned out to make my position even more untenable.

The door opened. The first person I noticed was a mature gentleman who, I deduced from his bearing, had to be the master of the house; beside him stood a woman who I instinctively knew must be Catherine Piggott. Tall and severe, she wasn't ugly in the strict sense of the term, but I defy any red-blooded male biped in the kingdom to find a shred of femininity there aside from her dress and her long ringlets. As for the steely sweetness of her smile, it sent shivers down my spine. Owen hadn't done me any favours, to say the least. She stepped across the threshold with a welcoming greeting:

'Achilles, you're here at long last –.'

And that was as far as she got, for the next second she slipped on the step and went flying, landing painfully on her posterior and clutching her ankle. Owen would have been proud of my impersonation of a caring fiancé when, a few minutes later and full of anxious solicitude, I helped Nicholas to install her in the carriage. Unfortunately, the confines of the carriage prevented me accompanying her to the doctor and probably to the hospital afterwards. After the lanterns of the carriage had disappeared into the night, I heaved a mental sigh of relief for having – at least for the moment – been spared the company of a "fiancée" who was scarcely the epitome of feminine charm. But my relief was short-lived as it dawned on me that her absence now placed me in a most precarious position. How could I mingle plausibly with the others without her there to steer the conversation towards our supposed relationship? And what had she already told them about "us"? I was completely in the dark.

The flurry of activity following the accident had not allowed any time for formal presentations. I entered the dining-room with my host and realised that I had already glimpsed two girls there -- presumably Daphne and Sibyl -- while I was helping Miss Piggott into the carriage. The young redhead, seventeen or thereabouts, was clearly not the bride-to-be; she must therefore be Daphne. Nor, as it turned out, was her sister Sibyl completely unknown to me. For I was only mildly surprised to recognise the young woman whom I had so frightened in a dark alley in London a year earlier.

4

THE LIGHTS GO OUT

Sibyl Mansfield pretended not to recognise me. But there was no doubt in my mind. There was no mistaking the furtive glances, the pursed lips and the naturally pale complexion. Undeniably my presence there disconcerted her, but it did not diminish her beauty: quite the contrary. She was like one of those perfect creatures that normally appear only in dreams; a fragile vision with a porcelain complexion, more translucent than even on the first occasion we met, but alive and infinitely desirable. Her long silky black locks were a feast for the eye and created an irresistible desire to run one's fingers lightly through them. So I was quite upset when that is precisely what Samuel Piggott did.

We were seated around the dining-room table and I was obviously the centre of attraction. I had already decided the best approach was to tell the truth as much as possible, while feigning an embarrassed shyness to avoid awkward questions about our relationship. Apart from a couple of expressions of concern for my "fiancée" and her prolonged absence, I steered the conversation to South Africa which quickly provoked passionate and lively discussion as I had anticipated. In all, I was quite satisfied with my tactics.

There were seven of us at table, in other words everyone in the residence except the servants and Mary, Nicholas's charming wife, who was exactly as he had described. A small blonde full of energy, she supervised the kitchen staff and, I was to learn later, the running of the entire household. Charles Mansfield himself was a gentleman of proud bearing, with rather long grey hair and a certain weariness in his eyes which, I suspected, was not entirely attributable to physical tiredness.

Daphne was even more slender than her sister, although clearly more energetic. She didn't take her eyes off me. Her eyes sparkled with the impish look of an adolescent. Her freckles and glorious red hair went marvellously well with her mischievous air.

Samuel Piggott was seated opposite me. A short, tubby fellow with a permanent smirk and piggy eyes, he appeared to be as completely at home as a contented cat, although once or twice I detected flashes of anxiety in those small eyes for no apparent reason. I could have imagined him in many different roles save one: that of Sibyl's husband. The very idea of such a marriage revolted me, it was so grotesque. He was well into his fifties whereas she was a flower which had only just begun to bloom. The reader will of course understand that I was at pains not to allow my feelings to show, given the circumstances.

To Piggott's left sat a curious individual, about whose existence Owen had neglected to inform me, and who had been introduced to me as Professor Julius Morganstone. Despite a roaring fire in the hearth, he seemed to be shivering under a large cape which he had apparently insisted on wearing at table. He was a strange fellow, with heavy-lidded protruding eyes staring out from under thick bushy eyebrows, and a long drab lock of hair partially covering his face.

Edgar Forbes, Piggott's business partner, seemed scarcely more likeable. Thin, in his thirties and taciturn, his lively and penetrating gaze nevertheless indicated that he was far from being short of grey matter.

We were in the midst of discussing the recent discoveries of gold ore in Transvaal when it occurred to me that Catherine Piggott may well have taken one of those present into her confidence, for I felt as though I was being watched. Was it Edgar Forbes? He seemed a likely choice. Unless it was Piggott. After all, what more natural than his own sister confiding in him? In any case, even though he might be laughing up his sleeve at present, any such confidant would know to keep a discreet silence. What's more, I had a distinct impression that nobody was at ease, even though in most cases there was nothing I could put my finger on other than a certain nervousness of gesture; the exception being Sibyl, whom I noticed repeatedly glancing out of the window.

When Forbes happened to mention that Nicholas had not yet returned, I mentioned the figure we had seen in the snow on our arrival.

There was a general intake of breath as everyone appeared to be seized by the same mixture of surprise and fear which had afflicted the coachman. When I explained whom we had seen, their anxiety changed to confusion and some even seemed quite upset.

'Harry Nichols, here? Wandering around outside the house? ' asked Charles Mansfield brusquely.

'He seemed to come from this direction,' I replied cautiously. 'I can't be more precise.'

'Extraordinary. It's three years since he last showed his face here. He could at least have rung the bell and said something.'

'He's already been here, father,' said Sibyl in a flat voice. The day before yesterday –.'

'What?' exclaimed Samuel Piggott. 'What audacity! What nerve! After the way he humiliated you.'

Sibyl replied, her eyes lowered:

'I had asked him not to come here again.'

'It seems that wasn't enough, my dear.'

It wasn't long before I knew much more of the story, although I'd already formed an opinion about Harry Nichols. As soon as the meal was over, the master of the house invited me into his study where I naturally expressed my concern about what had happened and my embarrassment at finding myself in such a situation.

'I'm very sorry, for if Catherine has to stay several days in the hospital, I fear I would be abusing your hospitality.'

'My dear Stock, you're our guest and it's out of the question that you would leave because of this unfortunate accident. Christmas is a wonderful time, full of joy, friendship, and nothing else. For several years we've spent it surrounded by our friends. It's the perfect time to forget all our woes and to get together purely for the pleasure of each others' company.'

He intoned the words as if he was trying to believe them himself, for it was obvious that a shadow was hanging over the proceedings. He treated me to a discourse about his ancestors, master drapers whose prosperity dated to Tudor times when they had built this enormous property whose upkeep was a continuous struggle, even for someone who owned two shops in London, made the best suits in the capital and enjoyed an impeccable reputation. A reputation, incidentally, which was due in no small measure to the efforts of his friend Samuel Piggott.

'Samuel is a friend of long standing, you see: someone one can count on and who has helped greatly these last few years, when business has not been easy. I must say how delighted I am that you've had the opportunity to make the acquaintance of his charming sister whose qualities I've come to appreciate over the years as our guest during the annual festivities. I expect she's already told you about the joyous event which will soon unite our two families?'

I felt it safe to admit that I was indeed aware.

Mansfield offered me a cigar and took his time lighting one for himself as well before continuing:

'I believe it to be a very good thing. It will be a very stable union, I'm quite convinced of that. The feelings Samuel has for my daughter are those of a mature man, that's to say noble, considerate, and constant. And it's no sudden infatuation: he's always had great admiration for Sibyl.'

'If I'm not mistaken, this Harry Nichols is an ex-fiancé?'

'Perfectly true, although that's rather too grand a word. He was really just a flirt. Nevertheless, he did manage to upset my daughter quite a bit by leaving the village so abruptly for who knows what reason. That was three years ago. We never saw him again until just now. Of course, that subject's taboo in front of Samuel, who –.'

'—who already had his eye on your daughter, if I've understood correctly.'

Mansfield nodded, seeming not to notice the impertinence of my remark, and continued in his monotonous voice:

'I remember the event well because it occurred only a couple of weeks before the tragic disappearance of Edwin. Miss Piggott has spoken of this to you, no doubt?'

I replied cautiously:

'She did make a vague reference to it.'

Mansfield seemed on the verge of pouring his heart out, but the memory must have been too painful, for he merely said:

'Naturally that kind of thing leaves its scars, and on none more than our poor Sibyl. She almost broke down. And the attitude of the idiot police didn't help one bit. At one point they practically blamed her for the crime. For almost a month she hardly opened her mouth. We feared the worst. Samuel tried his best, but to no avail. She did seem much better the following year, when she joined the Salvation Army.'

The Salvation Army! So that's what had brought Sibyl to the most squalid parts of London, where I had seen her for the first time.

'And then, a few months ago, when she agreed to marry Samuel, I realised that everything was going to be all right; she had fully recovered from her depression following Edwin's death. It's true: life isn't always a bed of roses, and I should know.' He gave a long sigh.

Charles Mansfield was clearly in the mood to share confidences although he had a tendency to beat about the bush. I did, however, learn that he had twice been a widower. His first wife had died while Sibyl and Daphne were both still in their adolescence. His second wife was herself a widow with a son, Edwin, the same age as Sibyl. The two sisters found themselves suddenly blessed with a brother and a new mother. But, alas! less than a year later she too died, taken by the same lung disease which had killed the first Mrs. Mansfield. And this despite all his efforts to save her, including an extensive sanatorium stay in the Swiss Alps, all of which had come to nought.

There was a knock on the door. It was Mary, come to announce that her husband had just returned, bringing the "bad" news that Miss

Piggott would be staying a few days in hospital with her leg in plaster. I arranged my expression to show the appropriate concern and, after Charles Mansfield had wished me a refreshing night's rest, I followed Mary, candle in hand, who showed me to my room where she had already prepared a soothing cup of herbal tea.

After having climbed the massive oak staircase which led up from the hall, we followed the wide corridor of the central section and then the narrower one of the west wing. Mary explained to me that this part of the house was not normally occupied. I had no difficulty believing it, for an icy dampness pervaded everything and even the permanent draught which was causing my teeth to chatter seemed incapable of ridding the place of a disagreeably musty smell. The flickering flame of the candle illuminated the occasional cobweb which had escaped the recent and cursory cleaning. The windows of the corridor were on the left side and overlooked a courtyard, in the middle of which I could see a moving lantern and recognised the imposing figure of Nicholas Dudley, no doubt on his way to check his horses one last time. Here where I stood all was silence, but for the floorboards creaking under our feet despite the protective carpet, and the insistent moaning of the wind.

Mary opened the door to a spacious and pleasant room where I was pleased to see a comforting red glow in the hearth.

I realise that up to now I have spent scant time describing the interior of the house, where wool reigned supreme in all its forms: either by itself or mixed with silk, cotton, or linen; in sumptuous curtains and in furniture covers, from the smallest stool to the largest sofa. The woodwork, too, was remarkable: for example the panels and mouldings in the dining-room, particularly around the windows, which would have delighted a certain Owen Burns of my acquaintance. Nevertheless, everything had a used and tired feel and I noticed here and there the occasional item in need of replacement. In the same vein, a residence of this size required more personnel than the two maids who were the only help the Dudleys had to run the place.

After lighting an oil lamp, Mary enquired when I wished to take breakfast and withdrew after turning down my bed. The clock over the mantelpiece showed almost ten o'clock. I went over to the window and became lost in contemplation of the barren and snow-covered landscape sparkling under the stars, where the sound of the wind was intensifying. In my mind I could see Sibyl's delicate and mysterious face. The first time I had seen her she had been in the grip of terror. She had even, for an all too brief moment, asked me to help her. And now she seemed to be in its grip once more, although more restrained this time. 'Which is not surprising given that she's about to marry someone old enough to be her father,' I growled, gritting my teeth. But of course there was something else, namely the story of the "white face" and the "tinkling bells."

The wind was still whistling loudly, yet it seemed to me that if I concentrated very hard I could convince myself I could hear a distant tinkling of tiny bells. It dawned on me that being confined to such a gloomy and melancholic spot could well induce feelings of depression. A shiver ran down my spine and for a long moment I thought about the disparate elements of murder, marriage, Christmas, tinkling bells and white mask.

Before going to bed, I decided to take one quick look at the corridor. I had nothing specific in mind, such as the detailed inspection of the neighbouring rooms. Just one quick look. Wasn't that my brief: watch and listen?

I went as far as the end of the corridor and stopped there for a few moments. Pressing my forehead against the nearest window, I concentrated on the wooden gallery which bridged the courtyard below at a height of seven yards and, for a brief moment, I imagined myself there behind one of the windows, following the hunt.

To my relief, there were no sounds of dogs barking, which was a good sign. I started back to my room. Casting a casual eye down at the courtyard, I could see the illuminated window of the drawing room and was somewhat surprised to see almost the entire household seated around a table. Suddenly, the light dimmed perceptibly leaving the flame from only one candle, which disappeared almost immediately. I racked my brains to no avail. I found myself utterly unable to explain what I had seen with my own eyes (or, rather, had not seen): *all the lights in a room had been extinguished while all the occupants were sitting around a single table!*

5

THE WHITE MASK

Seconds, then minutes, went by without anything happening. I was starting to feel numb from the cold. It was absurd. Surely someone would relight the lamps any second now. Someone *had* to. But no. Still nothing. After a while I was able to make out the faint red glow of a fire dying in the grate. A dim light which, at least in my imagination, accentuated the silhouettes of those persons still at table.

Try as I might, my eyes were unable to make out any detail so it was left to my imagination to determine what was happening. I waited patiently, rubbing my hands together and hopping from one foot to the other so as not to be frozen on the spot. I began to lose track of time and perspective, which was not very reassuring.

None of it made sense, I kept telling myself, and eventually I retired to my room angry, frustrated, and shivering with cold. A quick glance at the mantelpiece clock told me I had spent nearly an hour with my teeth chattering with nothing to show for it. It was only when I was under the bedcovers, which had retained at least some heat, that it occurred to me that I could have tried to get closer; but the warmth of the bed discouraged me from action and so in the end I doubted the evidence of my own eyes. I dreamt it. I *must* have dreamt it. Before I slid into the arms of Morpheus, Sibyl came to join me in my dreams.

A soft and gentle tinkling of bells brought me out of my dreams. It stopped as soon as I poked my nose out of the covers. It was still pitch black. What time was it? I knew there was nothing for it but to get up. I struck a match to see the time: one o'clock in the morning. The earlier scene came back to me so, after donning a dressing-gown, I went to look at the drawing room window. I stepped out into the corridor. The room was still plunged in darkness – which, at this time of night, was hardly unusual – but now I could see the reflection of a moving light in the courtyard snow.

I pressed my nose against the window. The light was coming from the floor below, just beneath where I was standing. And it was more than likely that someone was walking, candle in hand, along a corridor just like the one I was standing in. The flickering light continued for the length of the courtyard, and then disappeared.

There was nothing particularly unusual about it, but I decided to investigate anyway. I tiptoed towards the central staircase, which I descended just as carefully. Just as I reached the hall, I noticed a shaft of light at the end of the corridor. I crept towards it with even greater caution. The light was coming from behind the half-open door of a room on the corner of the central corridor and the west wing. On reaching it, I risked a cautious look inside. At first I only saw a comfortable room, albeit strangely furnished, but I soon realized this was where they stored the remaining vestiges of what had built the Mansfield's original wealth: a weaving loom; a spinning wheel; and various measuring and trimming devices hanging from the walls. I craned my neck to locate the source of the light and saw a candle on a small table to the left of the chimney…and saw Sibyl sitting calmly in a high-backed chair.

I pulled back.

I was fairly sure she hadn't noticed me as I carefully retraced my steps to the foot of the stairs, where I took up my observation post hidden behind the banister. I could detect the occasional faint noise, such as a wardrobe door opening and closing. What could Sibyl be doing at this hour of the night? I couldn't imagine; the brief glimpse I'd had of her was no help. There had been no hint of fear, fatigue, anger, or sorrow. Nothing. She had appeared as expressionless as a statue. A few minutes after I had hidden myself she left the room, closed the door quietly, and took the corridor leading to the west wing. There was the sound of another door closing and I found myself in total darkness.

I reached my room with a thousand questions in my mind, but was somehow able to fall quickly asleep quickly. But I was suddenly awakened again, and this time there was nothing soft and gentle about it: the scream of a terrified woman shattered the silence of the night.

I remained paralysed with fear for a couple of seconds. It was a truly blood-curdling scream. Also, it seemed to me that I could hear another voice as well. I jumped out of bed, grabbed my dressing-gown and rushed out of my room. I realised the screams had come from fairly close by, but it was the certainty they came from Sibyl that steered me towards the corridor I had seen her take not long before.

I took the stairs two at a time as the screams continued to ring out. Reaching the corridor in question, I saw Forbes in his nightshirt and nightcap, with a candle in one hand, trying in vain to calm Sibyl and Daphne who were both terrified and horror-struck, their faces as white as the nightshirts they wore. Nicholas arrived. Then the others.

'I saw him, I saw him,' moaned Sibyl. 'I saw his white mask through the window.'

'So did I,' declared Daphne, who seemed to be recovering. 'First of all I heard the little bells and then Sibyl's screams. It was only then

I saw a white shape behind the glass. It was horrible. It looked like a dead man.'

6

A WALK IN THE SNOW

Next day, in the early afternoon, Daphne and I found ourselves bouncing about in Nicholas' carriage and looking through the window at the wintry landscape as we headed towards the outskirts of the capital. It was a dry and sunny day, but cold nonetheless. Having risen rather late, I had missed Nicholas' earlier trip to Catherine's bedside, when he had taken Samuel Piggott and Edgar Forbes. Returning in time for lunch, they informed us that she had a maximum of three more days in hospital and was in high spirits, though they made a point of stressing how disappointed she had been not to have seen me. It was Forbes who was at pains to point it out, with a rather forced politeness.

It was a mere six miles or so from where Miss Piggott was recuperating and I couldn't, in all decency, avoid a visit. In any case, there were matters I wished to discuss with her with some urgency. So when Daphne made the kind offer to come with me I accepted graciously, even though I would have much preferred a quiet *tête-à-tête* with the invalid.

I watched my companion out of the corner of my eye as she bounced up and down on her seat. If I had had to compare her with one of God's creatures, I would have unhesitatingly opted for the grasshopper, for she was as light as a feather and perpetually on the move. The thought had struck me earlier in the day as we had been examining the traces of footprints around the house and I had had to catch her to prevent her falling as the consequence of a reckless slide. A grasshopper indeed, of a lively and cheerful temperament, and bursting with energy: a veritable coiled spring, incapable of staying in one place for any length of time.

In speaking of investigations, I am inevitably led to the events of the previous night. The two sisters had noticed a shadow falling across the window of their room, followed by a shape pressing its hideous pallid face against the glass for several seconds. Daphne, whose attention had been drawn by her sister's scream, also saw it; she thought she also heard the sound of tinkling bells. Those were the bare facts, to which not much could be added, given the suddenness of the appearance and the terror it inspired. Curiously enough, the rest of the household – Mansfield, his guests, and Nicholas and Mary – appeared to be equally as frightened by the mysterious apparition. Yet they accepted the incident with resignation, not even asking any questions – which would have been the natural thing to do. There had been furtive looks, heavy with meaning, passing between them, but few words spoken. I had come to the conclusion that they all shared a terrible secret, which no doubt lay at the heart of the investigation Owen had asked me to undertake. I had opted for discretion and circumspection, stoically resisting the temptation to bombard them with questions, but I was burning with curiosity to know why they had all been seated around a table in total darkness, and what Sibyl had been doing in the middle of the night.

Nevertheless, over breakfast, I had suggested to Daphne that we take a walk outside to look for any traces the intruder may have left under the sisters' window. In that way, I could demonstrate an understandable curiosity, while avoiding arousing suspicion by operating alone. And we did indeed discover a whole series of footprints – albeit somewhat blurred due to being repeatedly trodden over – extending the length of the west wall, seemingly those of a single adult individual with average-sized shoes. There seemed to be just as many footprints under the windows of the rooms adjacent to Sibyl and Daphne's, which was situated just under mine. They came from the road and returned there, and seemed in all likelihood to have been left by Harry Nichols, Sibyl's ex-fiancé, whom I had seen there as I arrived. But if that were the case, where were the footprints left by the apparition? The only reasonable conclusion was that the apparition and Harry Nichols were one and the same. I had made that same observation to Daphne, who had replied, strangely: 'I would love to believe you....'

'I say,' she said suddenly, looking at me with a mischievous gleam in her eyes, 'if we get back early enough, can we go for a walk in the snow?'

'A walk in the snow?' I replied, amused by this child who obviously considered me to be a friend after that morning's investigation. 'Well, why not be at one with nature?'

She pretended to clap at my remarks:

'Exactly! I love everything that's beautiful. I would have loved an artistic career --'

I thought I heard Owen's words echoing in my brain.

' – but my father won't hear of it. He says a woman's place is elsewhere.'

'What kind of artistic career?'

'In sports.'

Intrigued, I said nothing, but studied her physique in the hope of deducing what her chosen discipline might be. Head down, she fiddled with a finely chased silver ring on her right ring finger. Then she straightened up and declared proudly:

'Skating. Figure skating.'

"Has anyone ever seen a grasshopper on ice skates?" I said to myself, vastly amused; but I hastened to tell her solemnly that I was sure she possessed considerable talent. While continuing to complement her, I launched into a lecture on Art worthy of Owen Burns himself. Daphne listened with rapt attention and, I flatter myself, a degree of admiration. By the time we reached the hospital, I was confident that I had at least one ally amongst the Mansfield clan, but one who seemed utterly unable to understand – despite several heavy hints – that I wished to be left alone with Miss Piggott. Nevertheless, she did eventually decide to get some fresh air and leave us alone for five minutes.

As soon as the sound of her footsteps had receded, I leant towards Catherine and whispered:

'Quickly, tell me everything I need to know. I have no idea what I'm supposed to know and how I'm supposed to act with regard to our "engagement"; my friend has told me next to nothing.'

Nature had not been overly kind to Catherine Piggott, but I found myself liking her. There was something touching about her, confined to her bed, anxious and frightened. Her words came in a rush as she explained how my friend's letter had arrived barely a couple of hours before my arrival, telling her I was to replace him. She was fearful for the life of her brother, now that he was soon to become a member of the Mansfield family, and just before Christmas to boot. Only Edgar Forbes was aware of her recourse to a detective; her brother himself was unaware of the fact. That was all she was able to tell me, for Daphne had just come back.

On the way back Daphne, after staring at me for some time, declared:

'I got the impression you were trying to get rid of me.'

'Really?'

'Don't pretend, you can't fool me for a second. I know who you really love.'

I was startled and stammered:

'Who I really love? What are you talking about?'

'I saw you and Catherine back there and I'm quite sure you feel absolutely nothing for Miss Piggott. She's not the one who's taken your fancy.'

I could see it coming: she was going to tell me it was she I had fallen for. But her next words took me completely by surprise:

'You're in love with Sibyl. Don't pull such a face. It's perfectly obvious. She spoke to me yesterday, just before she went to bed.'

'You mean *she* told you that?'

'No. I keep telling you: you give yourself away by the way you look at her, as if you've never seen a woman before. By the way, let me remind you she's about to get married. Yes, Sibyl spoke about you and how you'd already met very briefly but she hadn't forgotten your face. She finds you....'

She left the words hanging in the air – deliberately. I realised as much when she simply shrugged her shoulders when I asked her exactly what her sister had said. There followed a long and awkward silence, during which I asked myself if Daphne was talking nonsense or whether I truly was in love with Sibyl. Which, if I were to be honest with myself, could not be ruled out.

Again, Daphne caught me off guard:

'Tell me, Achilles, do you know about the Lord of Misrule?'

'The what?' I repeated, startled – for the name did sound vaguely familiar. 'The Lord of Misrule? No, I don't think so.'

'That's what I thought,' she muttered. 'You don't know anything.'

She was really becoming irksome, and I asked her brusquely if she would care to enlighten me.

'Another time,' she replied, lost in contemplation of the shop window displays, each more tempting than the next.

It was just after four o'clock when we stepped beyond the hedges surrounding the Mansfield property. I was walking behind Daphne, still angry with her, but thankful I was wearing fur-lined boots. The "grasshopper" forged ahead energetically, warmly wrapped in a thick coat and wearing a woollen cap. We set off first in the direction of the village, then took a path to the left which headed towards open fields. There was a frozen crust on the surface of the snow and the only sound in the great white silence was that of our boots crunching through. The desolate monotony of the landscape was broken by the occasional skeleton of a leafless tree. Attempting to make conversation, Daphne observed that it hadn't snowed for several days. I pointed out that it was surprising, given that in the capital it hadn't let up the whole of the previous day.

'Surprising or not, that's what happened,' she retorted.

I sensed she was vexed, probably due to my long silence.

A little further on, she asked my help to overcome an obstacle she could well have negotiated on her own. A small stream of water had forced its way between some reeds frozen in the ice. She explained quite seriously that, before the extreme cold had set in, there had been an initial fall of snow which had caused the stream to overflow, and that the excess water had frozen in the subsequent chill.

I picked her up in my arms and stepped on the ice, which promptly broke, followed by a second step with the same result. We crossed the stream and slipped on the ice on the other side, throwing us both into the snow. The whole manoeuvre was idiotic because we could each have managed better on our own. Nevertheless, it made Daphne burst out laughing, clearly delighted my discomfiture and unhurt because her fall had been cushioned by your humble servant. She asked me if it was an attempt on my part to join Miss Piggott in hospital. I didn't appreciate the remark and made as much clear to her.

'So you do love Sibyl!' she said mockingly.

I had obviously given myself away, at least with regard to my feelings toward Miss Piggott. I was careful not to offer comment, and went on the counter-attack:

'And what do you think of your sister's fiancé? ' I asked.

She lowered her gaze and said nothing. My shot had struck home.

'Let me see,' I continued, determined to strike while the iron was hot. 'Your sister must be in her twenties, and her future husband must be at least twice that – he must be the wrong side of fifty. I've nothing personally against the fellow, but you must admit he's no Adonis and I don't understand what your sister sees –.'

'That's enough!'

She was clearly fighting back a more scathing remark.

'As far as I can see, your sister doesn't possess such an irresistible craving for riches that she would be willing to sacrifice the best years of her life. After all, her ex-fiancé was a fellow of fairly modest means.

After a long silence, punctuated by energetic strides in the snow, she eventually said:

'You know, Sibyl has suffered a lot....'

'Because Harry Nichols broke off their engagement?'

'No. I mean, yes: there was some of that. But it's most of all because Edwin was taken from us. Did you know Edwin? No, of course, you couldn't have done. It's funny... when he was there, the whole atmosphere of the house changed. He wasn't really our brother, but we loved him just as much as if he had been.'

'Your father told me about him.'

Daphne appeared not to have heard me.

'He was about your height, but slightly slimmer, with dark hair and a moustache... We loved him very much. Look!' She withdrew her hand from her muffler to show me her silver ring. 'He gave me this for my birthday. I was thirteen years old at the time, so it was a little large for me. He told me it was done on purpose, so that I would always be able to wear it and think of him.'

She shrugged her shoulders as if to shrug off the tears, then continued:

'He was always playing jokes on Sibyl, but he adored her. He even told her he would marry her one day. Then there was that terrible Christmas three years ago when he was murdered....'

'Your father told me about the tragedy,' I said gently. 'As I understand it, she was even accused of the crime herself. Is that right?'

'Yes, because she was the only one who could have done it. Or, at least, she was the best placed in purely practical terms. But the whole thing was eventually shown to be impossible, because nobody can jump three yards in the snow without a run-up.'

'Listen, I know next to nothing about the tragedy except some vague remarks Nicholas Dudley made on the way down here yesterday. I must admit I'm starting to get interested. As far as I know, the murderer was never arrested.'

'That kind of creature cannot be arrested.'

'*That kind of creature?* Do we know what kind?'

'Of course. It paid us a visit last night: The Lord of Misrule.'

7

THE LORD OF MISRULE

'The Lord of Misrule,' said Charles Mansfield in his laconic voice. 'Surely that rings a bell, Mr. Stock? I realise you've spent the best part of your life in South Africa and I can well imagine that Christmas is celebrated differently down there. Perhaps you've forgotten, but we British have a particular soft spot for Christmas.'

The drawing-room clock struck half past five. Mansfield, his two daughters and I had just finished taking tea together. Piggott, Forbes, and Julius Morganstone had already left. As the light of day faded, the feeble light in the room died gradually away and the fire in the hearth remained the only illumination in the room. Sibyl having installed herself on the sofa beneath the window and therefore with her back to the light, I sensed rather than saw her delicate features. Next to me, Daphne, her face still glowing from the promenade outdoors, had barely been able to contain her impatience waiting for the three others to leave so that she could observe, to my detriment: "Papa, can you believe that Mr. Achilles has no idea who it was that paid us a visit last night."

'But there was a time,' continued Charles Mansfield, 'that the festivities did not take the form they do today. Profane joys and pleasures held sway then. Two or three hundred years ago, it was the custom to sing, dance, laugh, and drink for several days in a row. And any family of importance, noble or not, would elect a "Lord of Misrule" whose role was to preside over the revelries and invent all kinds of diversion, the more depraved the better, with the help of several hand-picked accomplices.

'I imagine each place had its own customs. Here in the village and the surrounding area, the "Lord" was chosen and crowned with great solemnity. In those days, as I've already explained, our ancestors exercised considerable influence due to their undoubted wealth and many in the region were in their employ. In short, they were powerful and respected and could therefore indulge their fantasies to a certain extent. In fact, it was their younger generation and their wild friends who elected the Lord of Misrule, and a handful among them who served as the Lord's disciples. They dressed up in the most extravagant costumes: livery of yellow or green, embellished with scarves, ribbons, lace and jewellery; not forgetting the obligatory little bells sewn into their tights. They made horses and dragons and other grotesque figures out of cardboard and paraded around with them in the company of a handful of musicians, committing every kind of buffoonery on the way. To the sound of fifes and the rhythm of drums and bells they charged the crowd, brandishing cardboard monsters and waving multicoloured ribbons over their heads before heading for the church, with complete disregard for any of the faithful praying there, and thence to the cemetery where they feasted and danced into the night.

'It's not hard to imagine them engaging in their farcical behaviour. At least they called it farce, but anyone who failed to appreciate their shameful activities would find himself with his head under water or subject to a merciless beating.'

While he continued to stare ahead, he couldn't help a shadow of regret passing across his features. His voice took on a more confidential tone:

'But, of course, all that had to end badly, sooner or later. It was the year that Peter Joke was chosen by the Mansfields to be Lord. Whether it was because of his name or because he was one of those obliging fellows, too naïve or too respectful of his betters to offer any resistance, he offered no resistance to the mischief concocted by my ancestors. I take it you understand that it was the so-called disciples of the Lord who actually directed the festivities: the Lord himself was just a figurehead to lend authenticity to the proceedings. The "coronation" took place as planned. Custom demands that, each year, the Lord of Misrule adopts a different appearance. That Christmas, Peter Joke dressed up in a thick black cloak, tights decorated with tiny bells, and a grotesque mask on his face made from some kind of whitewashed dough which gave it a horribly leprous effect, by all accounts. The mass of tinkling bells announced his arrival from afar. His "court" turned out to be exceedingly demanding and cruel, subjecting him to various torments for several nights, right up to Christmas Eve.

'Not far from here, behind the house, is a lake which had frozen over completely that year. Everyone had partaken liberally and quite a few were drunk on that fateful Christmas Eve, which was to be Peter Joke's last. Nobody knows for certain what happened, but it seems that someone had the foolish idea to hold court in the middle of the frozen surface and the "Lord of Misrule" drowned when the ice broke underneath him. Whatever the cause, the tragedy shocked and horrified the villagers and particularly, as you would expect, the victim's family. The loud silence of the disciples was taken as an admission, with good reason. Nevertheless, the tradition must have remained unaltered, for the following year another "Lord" was elected. And that's when it all started....'

And Charles Mansfield started to enumerate:

'At first we thought it was a coincidence when one of the Mansfields present at the death of Peter Joke was found drowned on the banks of the lake the day after Christmas... even though a witness had seen him going towards the lake accompanied by an unknown person dressed in black but with a face as white as a sheet.

'The following year, at the same period, another member of the family was found in the same spot, his body lacerated by multiple stab wounds. There were no eye-witnesses, but several family members present on the night of the tragedy reported hearing the tinkling of tiny bells, apparently coming from the direction of the lake.

'It was the year after that when the Mansfields started to become really worried: a third family member was found, savagely stabbed, not far from the lake. And this time the killer, with his black costume and face as white as snow, was seen running away – accompanied by the sound of tinkling bells. He was followed for a while across the fields, but easily managed to get away from his pursuers, *who swore that he hovered above the ground like a bird as he skimmed the hedgerows.*

'From that point on, there was no stopping the rumours. It was the ghost of Peter Joke, the Lord of Misrule who prowled the lakeside at Christmas to take his revenge on the Mansfields.
The next year there was yet another victim – the fourth – and that's when the wise decision was taken not to celebrate Christmas according to the old family tradition. After that, there was a period of calm, although from time to time there was the occasional accidental death which aroused suspicion. They became less and less frequent, however, and by the turn of the century the curse had more or less been forgotten.'

When Mansfield stopped there was a strange silence. The corners of the room were increasingly obscured by lengthening shadows. Sibyl and Daphne sat silently watching the flames of the fire, whose gentle crackling accompanied the familiar ticking of the clock. I noticed Mansfield's deep sigh as he continued:

'But four years ago, the area became once again the scene of a savage crime, and one that was signed, so to speak. Halfway to the village, a poor fellow was discovered by the side of the road, mortally wounded. He'd been bludgeoned with incredible ferocity by someone or something using a cudgel or a rock. It was old George, a distant cousin who lived more or less as a recluse on a farm a few miles from here. He was found by two witnesses who arrived on the spot just after the attack. The first swore he caught a glimpse of the victim fighting against an invisible "something" as he came round the bend from the village where he lived. He also claimed to have heard a sound fading away in the distance, which may well have been that of little bells. The other witness, as he was leaving this very house, heard a distant, fast-receding noise and then saw a "dark form" disappearing rapidly in the darkness. They both reached the dying man at the same time, but were only able to hear his last gasp. The next day a farming neighbour of George's found his horse in front of its paddock in a sorry state: frightened, wounded and exhausted, as if it had been in an encounter with a raging bull!

'Had the Lord of Misrule come back to torment us and hound us? Even though we were badly shaken, we refused to believe it. Until the following year when our dear Edwin was murdered. At that point there was no possible doubt, *because it was proven beyond any question that the abominable crime could only have been committed by a creature not subject to the laws of gravity.* The year after that there were no serious incidents, although on several occasion a dark shadow was seen roaming the area... a shadow leaving in its wake the sound of tiny tinkling bells. Here, almost every one of us has seen that hideous white face peering at us from behind a window-pane, not once but several times. A vision as terrifying as it is fleeting. Last Christmas it was the turn of a young village butcher to die in horrible circumstances. He died in almost the same place and under the same circumstances as Peter Joke. A few days beforehand, he had announced to his friends that he intended to reduce the so-called ectoplasm to sausage-meat if he ever found it. He was frequently seen leaving his house at nightfall, armed with a whip, and not returning until dawn. But one morning he didn't come back. It didn't take long to find his whip in the middle of the frozen lake, next to a large hole in the ice which had traces of blood around the edges. The body was only recovered later, after it had become possible to drag the lake. There were several wounds, notably to the hands and arms. But it's starting to get dark... Daphne, could you light the lamps?'

The improved illumination chased the shadows in the room away, but did nothing to those in my mind which, on the contrary, were getting darker by the minute. What I had just heard was an astonishing narrative, bordering on the absurd, but Charles Mansfield's expression was too grave for there to be any question of a joke. Sibyl's face, which I could not look at without a tug at my heart, was also solemn. What would I not have done to make her smile? Her deliberately offhand manner didn't fool me and did nothing to dispel the atmosphere of gloom in that vast isolated residence, nor the silence which I proceeded to break deliberately:

'You spoke just now of a creature not subject to the law of gravity in connection with your stepson's death. I think I understand, but –.'

'There were no tracks in the snow,' interceded Daphne firmly, 'and there should have been.'

Charles Mansfield did not react, but simply watched as his elder daughter turned her beautiful blue-green eyes on me and continued:

'Not only was I the last person to see Edwin alive, but I was the only one who could have –.'

Her voice caught in her throat. She looked long and hard at me, her eyes full of tears. I saw in them an anguish which rent my soul. For an instant I though she might leave the room, but she regained her composure and said calmly to her father:

'You may feel free to tell Mr. Stock exactly what happened.' She smiled wanly. 'A wife-to-be must learn how to control her feelings, mustn't she?'

Mansfield smiled back: a smile full of bitterness. After a moment of reflection, he turned again towards me:

'You must understand that it's painful for us to recall the tragedy, which we have all tried to put out of our minds. But there are some memories that cannot be wiped out; particularly of an investigation where the police continued to insist obstinately that the murderer was a normal human being. I can recall precisely the details of that night, and in particular the testimony of the main witness, Miss Harman, the governess, whom I had hired two or three months earlier. She was a conscientious and cheerful young woman, although rather timid, and she left our employ shortly after the tragic event.

'It's true to say that the strange death of old George the previous year was making us all feel a little apprehensive, but we didn't really believe in the ghostly spirit that terrorized our forefathers. Samuel laughed openly about it and Edgar Forbes joined in the fun, but Miss Catherine was more circumspect. I don't know what Edwin thought, for we only saw him during the school holidays. His room was situated at the far end of the east wing. I need to take a few moments to describe the layout of the premises in some detail.

'You've noticed that each of the wings contains a long corridor leading south from the main part of the house towards the door of the last room in that wing. Each of those two rooms is much more spacious than any of the others. Edwin's, at the end of the east wing, has – like its counterpart in the west wing – three windows. One of them looks west across the interior courtyard, another faces south and the third faces east. The corridor door isn't the only way to get into the room; you can also enter through the tower built against the wall facing the courtyard. The tower is situated between the west-facing window and the end wall of the wing. In previous times the two towers led up to the wooden gallery which traverses the courtyard twenty feet above the ground, but a long time ago the staircase became dilapidated and had to be bricked up. So these days the tower serves as a small lobby with one door leading from the courtyard and the other into Edwin's room. In fact, if the corridor door is bolted on the inside, the only way to get into the room is from the courtyard, for access from the tower is effectively blocked off.

'So, going back to the tragedy itself... It was Boxing Day – we had celebrated Christmas the day before – and we were all suffering from too little sleep and too much food. Sibyl, my dear, you were the last person to see Edwin alive. Late that evening, he came to see you in The Workshop –.'

Somewhat taken aback, I repeated:

'The Workshop?'

'Mr. Stock, the room we call "The Workshop" is a small museum which displays our history in the art of weaving and the machinery that was used. But, more importantly, it housed our sewing circle: our nimble-fingered ladies,' he added, with a smile.

Sibyl responded with a tender regard, but Mansfield had already continued:

'Do you remember how he seemed, Sibyl? Was he overly joyful or was he too sullen?'

'He appeared quite normal.'

'And, when he left you around ten o'clock, did he give you any indication that was expecting any visitors?'

She looked at her father without appearing to see him.

'No. No more than Nicholas, who had come to see me a little earlier.'

'Very well. Let's skip the next two hours, during which nothing much happened except most of us went to our rooms. Miss Harman's was the last but one in the west wing. She walked back there, candle in hand, around midnight and was opening the door to her room when she heard a noise at the corridor window behind her. Turning round, she saw a face pressed to the window, a ghastly pale face so horrible that she dropped the candle. It had just started to snow and the moon was almost full so that the courtyard was well illuminated. Miss Harman was thus able to see the shape she had seen fading away as it seemed to leave the property. According to her, it was wearing a long black cloak and a hat, but she was unable to give any more detail than that. She was aware of the family history and the mysterious death of old George the year before, so she decided to wait in the darkness. A fortunate decision for, a quarter of an hour later, the figure reappeared. By that time heavy flakes were falling but she nevertheless recognised the furtive gait. She became very agitated when she saw it enter the east wing tower, which she knew could only lead to Edwin's room. A moment later she saw a light in the adjacent window. The curtains were almost drawn, so all she could see were shadows blocking out the light. After a while her anxiety started to fade as she began to believe it might be a visit from a friend. Nevertheless, she stayed at her post for an entire hour, hoping to see the figure re-emerge. The light was still visible in the window and the snow had almost stopped. During the whole time, she swore, she had never taken her eyes off Edwin's room.

'At that point she went to bed and fell quickly asleep, but was awakened again by a loud noise at about two o'clock in the morning. Going out once more into the corridor, she was able to see Sibyl, five or six yards from Edwin's room which she had been trying to reach, struggling with an assailant. Miss Harman let out a loud scream and opened her window. Only a few seconds had elapsed but the assailant had vanished leaving Sibyl alone and motionless, her arms above her head in a desperate attempt at defence, near the open tower door, from which light was streaming.

'Before describing the sad spectacle that awaited us in Edwin's room, I need to describe the state of the snow and the thickness of the layer that was mostly deposited in the hour when Miss Harman was watching. The witnesses are unanimous: the only footprints in the courtyard were Sibyl's, going from the main entrance to just over three yards from the tower. *There were no other footprints than hers, do you understand?*

'Samuel and I were the first to enter Edwin's room, leaving Miss Harman to look after Sibyl, who was bleeding from the mouth. Almost everyone had been awakened by the noise and the screams. The light from Edwin's room could be seen through its open west door and the open tower door. Edwin was lying in the middle of the room in the midst of an appalling disorder: broken bottles, overturned furniture, et cetera, et cetera. It was immediately obvious that there was little hope for Edwin: he was bleeding profusely from multiple stab wounds.'

Charles Mansfield rubbed his eyes as if to erase the dreadful image, then continued in a firmer voice:

'Let me say right away, because it's of capital importance – and Samuel can attest to it as well as I – the heavy bolt in the corridor door was firmly in place as far as it could go and all three windows were locked on the inside. There was, in any case, no possibility that anyone could have entered via one of the windows not under Miss Harman's surveillance, because the snow under there was unbroken and had been so for far longer than the window on the courtyard side, which was swept regularly. There were no marks whatsoever on the thick virgin crust. Before he expired, Edwin tried to say something which sounded very much like "Lord of Misrule." We were to learn later that a thrust to the stomach from a dagger or suchlike was almost certainly the cause of death. In any case, it was a weapon with a long, sharp and extremely thin blade, to judge by the wounds. It was never found.

'But where was the killer? Not in the room, anyway, because the only places to hide would be in the cupboard and under the bed. There were no trapdoors, hidden openings or secret passages as the investigative team was quick to point out. So how did the murderer get out? Up the chimney? Much too narrow. Through the open door? Maybe, but to do so he would have to be lighter than air! For, apart from Sibyl's, there were no other footprints in the snow: not near the door, nor anywhere else. And that's not altogether remarkable, for Sibyl's assailant – who had been seen by Miss Harman – hadn't left any marks in the snow either. It must therefore have been the same creature....'

8

A DOOR OPENS....

1

At the end of dinner – a morose affair where the clinking of cutlery against porcelain had replaced conversation – Sibyl and Daphne were the first to leave the table. The younger sister said off-handedly that they were to be found in The Workshop should anyone need to find them, but the insistent way in which she looked at me made it clear that her words were addressed to me. After having served the obligatory liqueurs, Charles Mansfield gave his considered opinion regarding the possibility of snow, which aroused scant interest among Piggott, Forbes, Julius Morganstone and myself. To my great satisfaction, Piggott decided to retire to his room: the fellow disgusted me with his hypocrisy and condescending airs which I suspected hid a deep concern. Professor Morganstone followed shortly thereafter, still taciturn and mysterious. A few moments later Mansfield himself left, leaving me to talk *tête-à-tête* to Edgar Forbes whose supercilious smile had irked me from the start. He was pulling on a cigar which he had lit with the same enjoyment he derived from his knowledge of the precariousness of my situation.

I decided to deny him the pleasure of playing cat-and-mouse with me, as he was so obviously preparing to do. So, with a pleasant smile, I quickly gave him a summary of my role, including that of a last-minute replacement for the original detective, but without providing any explanation about the latter event.

He stared at me for a while before saying, curtly:

'So you were aware that I knew!'

'Yes, Miss Piggott told me this afternoon.'

'What a grotesque idea!' he sniffed, pursing his thin lips.

'Hiring a detective?'

He shrugged his shoulders:

'Of course not. Although she could have talked to me *before* seeking out you or your partner. No, what's grotesque is the very idea of the two of you – she at her age and you at yours – and she decking herself out with a fiancé as young as he's unexpected. It's... Well, let's just say it's surprising. I told her as much, of course, when she informed me after the fact.'

'Anyway, everyone seems to have accepted it,' I declared with as much aplomb as I could muster.

'Do you really think so?' he sneered. 'I wouldn't be so sure if I were you. But no matter, that's not what concerns me.'

He seemed to be more upset than the situation warranted and it was only later that I was to find out why. With his dry and severe appearance and aquiline nose, Samuel Piggott's partner looked the model of efficiency.

'Mr. Piggott,' I continued, 'isn't aware of his sister's arrangement, is he?'

'No. She was afraid of his reaction, as proved by the fact she didn't inform him.'

'But why the devil not? What she did was perfectly praiseworthy. After all, it was in her brother's interest.'

'You know about the menace hanging over this house, I assume? And what sometimes happens here at Christmastime?'

'Yes, but it's only the Mansfield family which is cursed, isn't it?'

'A family which Mr. Piggott will soon join.'

'He's very worried about it, that's true. But why would his sister be afraid that he'd find out she'd hired a detective to protect him?'

Forbes seemed to be debating with himself but, after sizing me up carefully, he declared:

'Mr. Piggott has his own views about how to combat danger and he has already taken the steps he considers necessary. I rather doubt, as a consequence, that he would appreciate efforts from other quarters. At least, that's what Catherine thought and I'm inclined to agree.'

'Might one enquire what his steps were? After all, if he wanted to shed light on the matter, I can't see how anyone other than a detective... I've got it! Mr. Morganstone is a detective in disguise, isn't he?'

'You're getting very warm, Mr. Stock, although you're not quite there yet. Mr. Piggott has, in fact, engaged Mr. Morganstone, but his investigative methods are very different from your own.'

Edgar Forbes looked furtively around, even though it was obvious we were the only two people in the room, then whispered mysteriously:

'If you want to know more, be in the drawing-room at ten o'clock. I can't say any more right now. You can see for yourself....'

2

The clock in the corridor was striking nine o'clock when I entered the room in which I had observed Sibyl in the middle of the night. She was sitting in the same place on her high-backed chair – a quite remarkable mahogany Chippendale "Gothic" – busying herself sewing buttons on child's coat. She looked up when I came in, acknowledged me with a faint smile, and went back to her work. Daphne, seated in another corner, winked at me over the cover of a book she was reading. What a beautiful picture the two sisters made, their graceful silhouettes outlined against the golden flame of the fire. There was a peaceful serenity in the room which contrasted starkly with the frightening and impenetrable mystery which hovered like a black cloud over the Mansfield family. I sat down beside the ancient spinning-wheel, feigning interest in its workings.

'You haven't told us yet what you think of the Lord of Misrule,' Daphne blurted out after a few minute's silence. 'Yet you seem very interested....'

'It's – it's quite incredible,' I replied, silently congratulating the "grasshopper" for bringing up the subject I most wanted to discuss. 'It's an astonishing story and I don't quite know what to say about it. I confess I don't usually have much truck with the idea of ghosts. But what do you think? You've seen the white face with your own eyes as recently as last night. What exactly does it look like?'

'There's no doubt in our minds about the ghosts, Mr. Stock,' declared Sibyl in a voice utterly devoid of emotion. 'As for the white face, I can only say it's quite horrible.'

'The only human aspect is the shape,' added Daphne. 'Try and imagine a deathly white face that looks as though it's been roughly thrown together from different parts.'

'And each winter it's the same. He lurks behind the windows and only shows himself when you least expect it. And you can hardly catch even a glimpse because he disappears as quickly as he's come.'

'But all the same, you must have got a good look at him that night when he attacked you.'

Sibyl put down her embroidery and I noticed her hands were trembling slightly.

'No, I didn't see anything, because I can't remember anything.'

'You can't remember anything?'

'I can remember that the door leading to Edwin's room was open and there was light streaming out on to the snow. I can remember hearing noise, lots of noise. I can remember that my arms and legs were hurting as if someone had struck them. And I can remember Miss Hartman calling out to me or shouting at someone. I can remember all that, but not what happened *beforehand*.'

'But nevertheless you did cross the courtyard.'

'I know. And that was what puzzled the police the most. They found it hard to believe I was sleeping.'

'That you were – but –.'

'My sister has been known to walk in her sleep,' offered Daphne.

'Ah, yes. I understand. I understand completely.'

Sibyl was a sleepwalker and I was a complete imbecile for not having realised that the night before. Yet her expression and her bearing should have made it obvious at the time.

'The police thought it was an excuse,' continued Sibyl. 'Some sort of trick to justify my presence there.'

'You can't really blame them, you know,' said Daphne. 'Edwin had just been mortally wounded, the weapon had vanished along with the murderer, and where you would have expected to see his footprints on the snow, there were only yours, Sibyl. But luckily for you, you stopped some way from the door. Otherwise, a few more footsteps, and I don't know what would have become of you.'

'So what did happen? Don't forget the testimony of the governess who saw you struggling with someone who must obviously have been the murderer. Let's see now... the killer has just committed his horrible crime and is running away when he suddenly finds you in his way. Not realising you're sleepwalking, he thinks he's been discovered and all is lost. He throws himself upon you to silence you for ever but, suddenly noticing the unexpected presence of the governess, he flees without finishing the job.

'The only problem,' I concluded, pitifully, 'is that he didn't leave a single trace on the snow.'

'One of the policemen even tried jumping the three yards from where Sibyl was standing to the tower door and almost succeeded. It had to be a standing jump, because her footprints showed she had been walking normally. However in the opposite direction he failed completely, in the sense that he was unable to jump without sliding forward and leaving traces on the snow that contrasted with Sibyl's orderly footprints. So, after their experiments, they concluded that Sibyl must somehow have taken a gigantic leap to leave the scene of the crime.'

There was a pregnant silence, which I broke by asking Sibyl rather stupidly what she was doing. She explained patiently that the little coat she was mending would go to some unfortunate child in one of the poor quarters of the capital, and that she spent a good part of her time repairing clothes collected from various parish donations, after which she went round with the Salvation Army distributing them. Needless to say, there was a great deal of work to be done around the Christmas period. After she had got up in order to show me two cardigans she had knitted for a pair of twins from an impoverished family, Daphne observed:

'They remind me of the one which disappeared that time. Did you ever find it?'

Sibyl blushed furiously:

'No, never. Someone must have stolen it. The same person who stole Nicholas's greatcoat.'

I raised an inquisitive eyebrow.

'On the day of Edwin's death,' explained Daphne, 'my sister had been doing some knitting and the next day it had disappeared.'

Sibyl had returned to her seat. A distant look came into her eyes and she spoke in a faint voice:

'I was sitting right here and had been working for some time on it when I started to lose count of the stitches. Nicholas came in. He had just come back from London and wanted to know when he was supposed to take me in next. As he was leaving, Edwin came in to talk to me about... about... I don't remember any more.'

'It was about Piggott. I remember hearing you. You were speaking in quite a loud voice.'

'Please, Daphne,' murmured Sibyl in a scarcely audible voice. 'It was the last time I ever saw him. What were we talking about? Oh, yes, in the evening of the next day I had come back here after all those horrible interrogations, but I couldn't find my knitting. I didn't really attach much importance to the loss, but I did find it surprising, all the more so when Nicholas complained about having lost his greatcoat.'

'And were they ever found?' I asked.

'No, not as far as I know. Compared with what else happened, it was relatively insignificant.'

Daphne stood up suddenly and left the room, ostensibly because she found her book too dull and needed to find another.

Her absence or, more accurately, the fact of being alone with Sibyl, stirred a great emotion within me which, looking at Sibyl's pale face, I could see was reciprocated. A sudden intimacy had been created between us, of which we were both perfectly conscious. I told her I recollected everything about our first meeting the year before in the dingy Aldgate street. She nodded her head slowly and said she remembered it clearly. I stood up and moved closer towards her:

'But why were you so afraid? I had the impression it was somehow because of me.'

'You did frighten me, but it wasn't your fault. You were wearing a strange hat, and you had snow on your face. And just before that, I had heard the tinkling of tiny bells, which must have come from a pony somewhere, but... anyway, I think you understand now. For a brief moment I though you were ... The Lord of Misrule.'

Her beautiful blue eyes looked up at me, without reproach. She was still afraid, but that was not the only reason her slender throat was choking with emotion beneath her silk blouse.

'As I recall,' I said as I took her hand in mine, 'you asked me to help you.'

She made no effort to pull her beautiful pale hand away and I caressed it for a moment before bringing it up to my lips. Just at that moment, the door behind us groaned and I turned quickly round to see the imposing silhouette of Samuel Piggott framed in the doorway.

9

'SPIRIT, ARE YOU THERE?'

It was gone quarter past ten when Daphne extinguished the lamps, plunging the drawing room into semi-darkness. We were all seated, fingers pressed down, around a table, with the flames from the hearth as the sole source of light. Although round in shape, it was not a pedestal table, having four slightly curved legs which gave it solid support. Despite its relatively small size, we had managed – Charles Mansfield, his two daughters, Samuel Piggott, Forbes, Julius Morganstone, Mary and myself – to place ourselves around it without being too cramped. Only Nicholas was absent – the day ahead of him threatening to be as arduous as today had been, he had gone early to bed. The surface which our fingers touched was not smooth; an elegant wood sculpture caused it to have a slightly raised surface pattern.

It wasn't hard to work out what we were doing and what had so intrigued me the night before, nor to deduce the role of Julius Morganstone, self-styled medium and, according to Samuel Piggott, one of the best in the capital.

'When it comes to summoning the spirits, Professor Morganstone has no equal,' he had explained to me earlier on while the aforementioned professor stared at me from beneath bushy eyebrows. 'That, in fact, is why I retained his services. Incidentally, I should tell you he has already presided over several such events on behalf of His Majesty, not to speak of numerous and precise indications given to the Yard during several particularly tricky investigations.'

'Wherever we are, wherever we go,' Morganstone had declared in a solemn voice, there are always spirits who may manifest themselves in one way or another. They are the sole witnesses of what we mortals are unable to see. And they are never wrong.'

'Nobody but he can help us unravel the two hundred year old mystery,' Piggott had continued. 'What really happened to the Lord of Misrule? Is it he or someone else who has set himself against the Mansfields? Is it he who has come back to stalk us once again? Who killed Edwin? And how was he killed? Those are the questions we are all asking, which obsess us, and which will surely be answered shortly for we have already been heard by those beyond.'

Which is how I learnt that they had made contact with a certain "Peter," but didn't know whether it was truly Peter Joke, the original Lord of Misrule, or not.

I was therefore intrigued to join them, and rather ill at ease, more because of my audacious conduct earlier that evening than by the experience itself, which I found hard to take seriously. Did Piggott, when he entered the "Ladies' Workshop"— as I had taken to calling it – realise that I was not immune to Sibyl's charms? Nothing, at least in what he said, indicated as much, for he had invited his fiancée in a perfectly natural voice to play draughts with him. But I thought I detected his smile to be forced and not at all amicable. Were my feelings as apparent as Daphne had claimed? If that were the case, then Samuel Piggott would have a double reason to despise me, for not only was I attempting to seduce his future wife, I was also making a fool of his sister Catherine.

I was deep in thought when the voice of Julius Morganstone broke the silence:

'Peter, are you there? We're waiting for you. We want to talk to you.'

Several minutes went by without any response to Julius's questions. I didn't know how "Peter" had made himself known on previous occasions, but it didn't take long for me to find out. A gentle knock shook the table. A knock which anyone could have made with their knee. So began the dialogue with "Peter," who responded to Morganstone's questions with a single knock for a positive response and silence for a negative. It was impossible for me to determine which of my neighbours was hitting the table with their knee – for I was certain that was the subterfuge being used – but, truth be told, it was of little importance to know whether it was Morganstone himself, an accomplice, or simply a joker. What interested me was the dialogue itself.

'Have you something to tell us?' asked Julius Morganstone.

A single knock.

'About the Lord of Misrule?'

Another knock.

A wave of anticipation swept through those present.

'Can you tell us something about him?' continued Morganstone.

Silence.

'Is he still alive?'

Silence.

'Is he dead?'

Silence.

'I don't understand,' confessed Morganstone, his brow now covered in perspiration. 'Peter, can you tell us if it was he who attacked the young butcher last year?'

Silence.

'Obviously he doesn't know,' mumbled the medium. 'Unless he's gone.' He cleared his throat. 'Can you tell us more about Edwin? Was he a victim of the Lord of Misrule?'

Silence.

'Of someone else?'

A knock.

A murmur of surprise swept round the table.

'Edwin was killed by someone other than the Lord of Misrule, is that what you mean?'

A knock.

'Do you know who it is?'

Silence.

'Peter, are you still with us?'

Silence.

'Is it someone else?'

A knock.

Morganstone nodded his head slightly and said in a solemn voice:

'Peter has gone and someone else has taken his place... or chased him away. This kind of substitution happens fairly frequently And it also explains the lack of precision in the responses. The first thing to ask him is who he is. We'll use the alphabetic method. A... B... C....'

The first knock occurred after the letter P. The operation was repeated until the letter I. After that there was a G, followed by another G, at which point everyone assumed it was the name PIGGOTT, which turned out to be the case.

Surprise could be seen on every face, and particularly on that of the person named, who stammered:

'But that's absurd! It can't be me. I'm here, as you can all see!'

'Maybe it's you he wishes to speak to,' said Morganstone gently. 'Maybe he has a message for you.'

The medium put that question to the spirit, who answered "yes." We started once more with the alphabetic method, which elicited T... R... U... T... H.

Truth.

'You have a truth to reveal to Mr. Piggott, is that it?' asked Morganstone.

A knock.

'The truth? But which truth? The truth about the mystery?'

Silence.

'About the mystery of the Lord of Misrule?'

Silence.

'About Edwin's death?'

A very sharp knock, followed by a deathly silence, after which several people started to speak at once and Morganstone restored calm with some difficulty. He was, however, unable to rekindle any kind of dialogue with the "spirit," who failed to reappear despite numerous prompts. When the oil lamps were re-lit, they showed nothing but perplexed faces.

'The mystery of the death of Edwin,' repeated the rich businessman, thoughtfully, playing nervously with his watch chain with one hand while the other clutched one of Sibyl's, the contrast between her long, fine fingers and his short pudgy ones being only too evident. 'Why the devil did he want to talk to me in particular?'

'Yes, why to you in particular,' echoed Sibyl, discreetly withdrawing her hand. 'That's certainly curious.'

'In any case,' declared Charles Mansfield, 'we can't afford to miss any opportunity to solve this mystery. Mr. Morganstone, do you think we shall be able to renew contact with this spirit?'

The professor pushed away the grey lock of hair in front of his eye and replied:

'Certainly. He didn't intervene for no reason, that's obvious. But we have to be patient. These manifestations can't be done to order. Perhaps he'll tell us more tomorrow evening.'

'We should perhaps ask him if there's a new danger threatening us.'

Mary spoke these words as she stood slightly apart from us, in front of the handsome glass-fronted bookcase next to the chimney. From where I sat I couldn't see the reflection of her eyes in the glass, but something in her voice told me that her words had something to so with the object of her attention.

It was only on the next day, in the late morning, just after I received a telegram from Owen asking to meet me later that afternoon in the village inn, that I happened to glance at the shelf of the bookcase where Mary had stood the night before. Apart from several lovely pieces of porcelain, there was a wallet embroidered with gold threads, a spectacle case in mother-of-pearl, and a dagger almost as long as a short sword and apparently of Spanish origin. The handle and the hilt were finely chiselled but it was above all the sharpness of the scintillating blade which drew my attention.

10

OWEN'S INSTRUCTIONS

The sky was darkening as I left the Mansfield residence, headed in the direction of the village. My throat was still sore from having gulped my tea down too hastily, so impatient was I to see Owen. My impatience had not escaped Daphne's eye and the situation was further compounded when I stupidly announced I was going out to take the air, after which I was only able to escape with great difficulty.

At the edge of the property I ran into Edgar Forbes who, hunched down in his coat with his hat jammed down over his eyes, was walking as fast as he could. He excused himself briefly and replied incoherently to my question as to whether he had come from the village, then disappeared into the courtyard.

I was too preoccupied myself to bother about his peculiar behaviour and, pressing ahead as fast as I could, pushed open the door of the pub a quarter of an hour later. The saloon bar, with its rustic décor and low ceilings supported by blackened old beams dating from centuries past, was deserted but for two customers at the far table. Owen Burns, wearing a faded tweed suit with a deerstalker hat set at a rakish angle – an outfit carefully chosen for effect, as I was beginning to understand – was chatting to an individual not entirely unknown to me: Harry Nichols, Sibyl's ex-fiancé. I sat down not far away, pretending not to know them. Owen sat there, not saying a word, content to nod his head from time to time at what his companion was saying which, as far as I could make out – for he was speaking very quietly – was a vehement diatribe. Five minutes later Nichols got up, said goodbye to Owen, and left.

'Now there's a young man singularly devoid of a sense of humour' said Owen as he watched the door slam while I sat down next to him. 'Just like all jealous lovers,' he added.

I explained who was involved.

'As I had more or less deduced, my dear Achilles. In any case, he doesn't seem to appreciate his replacement at all.'

'Piggott?'

'Yes. It seems that there were a number of dirty tricks played in order to get him out of the way. But I found it difficult to follow because he was clenching his teeth in anger.'

'Have you been waiting long?'

'Since five o'clock. But don't worry, there have been plenty of distractions. Nichols waylaid me straight away, just as one of his friends left him – and nearly knocked me over on his way out. He seemed in a great hurry.'

The last remark reminded me of the incident with Edgar Forbes, whom I described to Owen. It did seem that he was the individual in question.

'Curious,' I said. 'I can't quite see what Mr. Piggott's business associate would have to do with Harry Nichols. Unless he was carrying a message from Piggott warning Nichols not to have anything further to do with the Mansfields and most particularly with Sibyl.'

'Yes, yes, that's all very well. But tell me how you've been getting along, Achilles, and give me a complete account of everything your eyes and ears have taken in.'

For the next half-hour, Owen didn't open his mouth – no mean feat for an incorrigible chatterbox such as he – listening with careful attention to my detailed account of everything I had witnessed since my arrival.

'Remarkable, Achilles, quite remarkable. You've conducted yourself with considerable flair and imagination, particularly since your path was strewn with pitfalls and setbacks such as the broken ankle which removed your one and only ally from the scene. But you not only overcame that obstacle, you were even able to take advantage of it.'

I emptied my glass with a certain amount of satisfaction, even though I was under no illusion about the sincerity of my friend's flowery compliments.

'By the way,' I said, 'you didn't tell me about Professor Morganstone.'

'Miss Piggott spoke of him, but I didn't think he would be on the spot so quickly. You know, Achilles, this business landed in my lap without any time to think. I only met Miss Piggott twice and then only last week. Now, tell me what you think about this extraordinary business.'

'Edwin's murder?'

'No, we'll get to that later. I mean the whole affair.'

'I don't know what to make of it, I really don't. It seemed obvious at first that what had been happening had no rational explanation. But then there was the séance with the turning table, and frankly I'd be amazed if there were an avenging spirit involved. And what about the message for Piggott, where the circumstances of

Edwin's death were to be revealed to him? First of all, does anyone really know the precise details of the tragedy? And, if so, why reveal them to Piggott alone? To warn him of the risk he runs by being accepted into the Mansfield family? I have the greatest suspicion of those supposedly of good faith who use communication between the living and the dead to transmit their message.'

'Excellent, Achilles, excellent. You're reasoning like a seasoned professional. I can only congratulate myself again for having called on your services.'

Damn that Owen! Was he expecting me to roll over and purr while he tickles my stomach?

At that point, Owen went to replenish our glasses. When he returned, there was a worried look on his face.

'I must tell you, Achilles, that this latest turn of events disturbs me. I'll bet you anything that something's brewing. But what? If only I –.'

'Yes?'

'— if I could be personally on the spot. But it would be very difficult to put everything into reverse at this stage, as you well know. We couldn't very well persuade people that Miss Piggott had changed fiancés....'

'Quite. Already, the business about her fiancé appears surprising, if not suspect.'

'We're stuck, Achilles,' said Owen bitterly.

'You're telling me! We can't go back,'

Owen looked me straight in the eye. 'There's something you're not telling me. I know! You've fallen for Sibyl. That's it, isn't it? You're playing a dangerous game there, my friend. Don't forget you're engaged to Miss Piggott. Speaking of whom, when does she return?'

'Tomorrow. We saw her this morning.'

'And Christmas is the day after. Achilles, from now on you must be doubly vigilant. Try to find out at the next séance who's playing the part of the knocking spirit. It's very important. His identity will clarify much of what's happening.'

'Right-ho, but I can't guarantee anything.'

'For my part, I'll try and find out as much as I can about the little world you're living in. Don't look at me like that, Achilles. I did find time to make some enquiries. Please don't think that I've spent all of the last forty-eight hours in the arms of – no, I have my dignity, after all.

'Regarding Julius Morganstone, I know nothing more than anyone else in London. He's a clairvoyant, well regarded in high society, and there's no indication that he's a charlatan.

'Charles Mansfield owns two department stores in town which have both seen better days. He's the last descendant of a family whose fortunes have steadily diminished over the last two or three generations and it would be surprising if he weren't soon forced to sell part of his holdings. The only thing that could save him would be –.'

'— the marriage of his daughter to Piggott,' I concluded, clenching my fists.

'Precisely. Samuel Piggott himself is far from insecure. He owns several warehouses in the docks; he's one of the principal importers of fine fabric, particularly those from India. It appears that it's only because of certain business favours that Mansfield is able to stay in business.'

'I'm beginning to get the picture,' I said, scarcely able to recognise my own voice. 'The bastard is blackmailing the family: either he marries Sibyl and the Mansfield family regains their prosperity or... they face ruin.'

Owen shrugged his shoulders:

'You're very naïve, my friend. That kind of deal is common amongst even the most respectable families. Having said that, it's only speculation, but I believe it to be well founded. I trust you to get to the bottom of it. Allow me to proceed. Edgar Forbes has been working for Piggott for nearly ten years. Starting as a humble clerk, he worked his way rapidly to the top due to his perseverance. He's now Piggott's right hand man and he more or less runs the show. Piggott merely keeps an eye on things. As for his sister, there's not much to say except that she's still unmarried, which you already know. I would add that she's a sensitive person, well-educated, and full of tenderness for someone who understands how to please her.'

'If she has all those virtues, what are you waiting for?'

'She's your fiancée, dear boy, don't forget that.'

'Owen, I can't imagine what's holding me back.'

'Now, now, enough of that. I fear the fair Sibyl is causing you to lose your sense of humour. Let's not lose sight of what's important. As far as the Lord of Misrule is concerned, I've only been able to dig up facts about the most recent tragedies. The legend itself is too ancient to be of any use. There are precious few details about the murder of old George four years ago. The coroner described it as a simple prowler's crime to one of his friends. The murder of the young butcher last year, although receiving quite a bit of attention, yielded little at the inquest, the only certainty being that he ended his days in the lake. Which brings us to Edwin's murder, which is a horse of a different colour. The circumstances of his death were so extraordinary that they finished up in Scotland Yard's lap. And, as you well know, I have friends there.'

Owen withdrew an envelope from his jacket and placed in front of me. He lowered his voice as he spoke:

'All the essentials are here. I summarized where it was appropriate, reproduced to the letter certain statements, and concluded with a number of observations. You'll see for yourself. Read it with a clear head and we'll talk about it later. For now, I'll just make one observation. Unless the crime is the work of a phantom, it must have been committed by someone inside the household; someone living there at the time, because all around there was nothing but virgin snow free of all footprints. I would add that it was the work of an artist. I've been sure of that from the outset, or I wouldn't have bothered myself with the affair. I repeat, Achilles, an artist. Take note of it.'

'And the "artist" in question wears a carnival mask in order to scare people at night?'

'And why not? Would a vulgar criminal think of that?'

'But why, in Heaven's name? He's been playing his little game for three years, as far as I can tell.'

Owen stared at his glass.

'I don't know. In any case, there's danger in the air.' He turned suddenly towards the window. 'I'm waiting for a carriage. That must be it.'

'What? You're leaving already?'

'I must, my dear friend. I'm expected.'

'So when are we to meet again?'

'I'll contact you. And feel free to get hold of me if you think it's really necessary.'

He stood up, put on his overcoat, and adjusted his hat carefully.

'I shall think about what you've told me Achilles, you can count on that. Meanwhile, remember my advice. But above all, do everything you can to unmask the "knocking spirit." It's probably not the person who killed Edwin, for one can hardly imagine him confessing in such a manner and least of all to Piggott. So it's probably someone else; someone who, if they don't know every detail, must at least have general idea. And the fact they want to talk to Piggott intrigues me enormously.'

11

AN IMPOSSIBLE CRIME

It was after eleven o'clock when I reached my room. After poking the fire and throwing on another log, I settled down in the armchair with Owen's unopened letter in my lap. Basking in the pleasant warmth – most welcome after navigating the freezing stairs and corridors – I allowed myself a moment's respite while I went over in my mind the events of the latest "evocation of the spirits," which had taken place, just as on the previous night, in the drawing room and with the same participants. Despite my vigilance, I had not been able to determine which of them was playing the role of the communicating spirit. At first I had suspected Piggott himself, before realising that he was himself flinching in response to the knocks, as were the others, incidentally. I got the impression that Julius Morganstone had nothing to do with them, but it was only an impression. In any case, whoever was responsible was concealing his hand well. To be blunt about it, my efforts had been in vain.

The séance itself had confirmed the message transmitted to Piggott the night before regarding the truth about Edwin's murder. This time, however, the "spirit" had asked the rich businessman to hold himself at the ready, for a rendezvous would be arranged shortly, at which the "truth" would be revealed. At the end of the séance, Julius Morganstone was warmly congratulated by Charles Mansfield who pledged his undying gratitude if he succeeded in shining a light on the cruel mystery, an event which did indeed seem imminent. Edgar Forbes agreed with an equal fervour and Mary, fascinated by the medium, appeared unable to keep her eyes off him. Sibyl and Daphne appeared more muted in their appreciation. Meanwhile Piggott, although joining in with the others, appeared nervous and even anxious. He was to "hold himself ready" for what? Morganstone had explained that, because it was Piggott who had first asked the question, it wasn't surprising that the spirit wished to address him personally. He went on to say that it wouldn't hurt if Piggott appeared less suspicious in future if he truly wished the aforementioned light to be shone. Mansfield also chimed in: 'Samuel, I don't understand you. You seem hesitant and doubtful, just at the point where we're about to achieve our goal. Just when we've been offered an unhoped-for chance to free our family from the curse!' Piggott was forced to admit, albeit with a bad grace, that his attitude was stupid.

Owen's parting remark was still fresh in my mind, so I, too, found Piggott's attitude strange. But I have to confess that my feelings towards Piggott were far from being impartial. Love is blind, they say, and I was beginning to realise the truth of that cliché, for each time I thought about Piggott, I was unable to do so objectively. A few minutes earlier, I had felt an electric current flow through me as I watched him take her delicate hand in his pudgy fingers as he wished her goodnight.

My mind lingered on the scene as the deep moaning of the wind rose suddenly to a Wagnerian intensity. I shook myself with a start and opened the envelope.

It contained a dozen or so pages. The first of these contained a summary of the affair, not unlike what Charles Mansfield had told me, so I see no point in reproducing it here. A plan of the ground-level was included, together with a recapitulation of the movements of the principal players, in particular those of Edwin himself.

8.30 p.m. End of dinner. Sibyl and Daphne withdraw. Mansfield, Forbes, Edwin and Miss Piggott retire to the drawing room.

9.30 p.m. Nicholas Dudley has just returned. He goes to the "Ladies' Workshop" where he finds Sibyl. As he leaves, he runs into Edwin, who seems perfectly normal.

10.00 p.m. Edwin leaves the "Workshop." According to Sibyl, who is quite firm on this point, there was nothing to indicate he had a nocturnal rendezvous planned. He is never seen alive after that time. It was about then, or possibly slightly later, that everyone but Mary and Nicholas Dudley and Miss Harman, the governess, went to bed. The Dudleys busy themselves putting some of the furniture back in place and the governess, who is not sleepy, picks up the Emily Bronte novel which she has been enjoying and starts to read.

12.00 midnight. The Dudleys have just reached their room, and Miss Harman is the last to retire. The house is in darkness. She sees the white mask pressed against the window opposite the door of her room. It starts to snow.

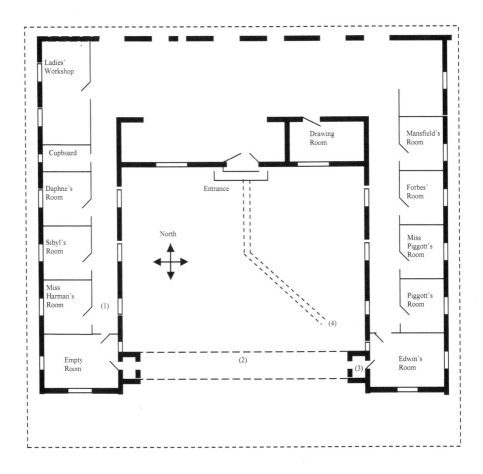

GROUND FLOOR PLAN

(1) Where Miss Harman was standing when she saw 'the shadow'
(2) Wooden gallery linking the two towers 20 ft above ground level
(3) Tower leading to Edwin's room, into which 'the shadow' vanished, as seen by Miss Harman
(4) Where Sibyl's footprints stopped

0.15 a.m. Miss Harman sees the shadow, which had vanished earlier, suddenly reappear and vanish again through the tower door leading to Edwin's room. It is now snowing heavily.

1.15 a.m. Miss Harman, who has been keeping watch on Edwin's room all this time, finally goes to bed. The snow stops.

2.00 a.m. A loud racket wakes the household. Miss Harman is first on her feet and, from the corridor window, she sees Sibyl in the courtyard fighting off an attacker. By the time she has opened the window and cried out, the attacker has vanished.

Before proceeding to extracts from the numerous police interrogations, my dear Achilles, I shall dwell for a moment on the question of footprints in the snow, which were inevitably affected by the various witnesses to the tragedy. Yet a careful examination by the police experts allowed us to retrace the steps of everyone involved. First, there were Sibyl's, which were quite clear. They went from the main entrance, across the centre of the courtyard, then angled slightly in the direction of Edwin's room and stopped three yards short of the tower entrance. Then there were Miss Harman's, which followed the same path as Sibyl's as she went to help her, after which they both turned and went back to the main entrance. Piggott and Mansfield were the first to discover Edwin's body in his room. Luckily they realised immediately the importance of the virgin snow around the tower and were careful not to mix their footprints with the others and to make sure nobody else got close. As for the footprints themselves, the police are certain they haven't been tampered with, such as by obliterating a small footprint with a larger one. There's no doubt about the duration of the snowfall: between midnight and one o'clock, confirmed not only by Miss Harman but by several villagers. The police estimate that nobody could have crossed the courtyard after half past twelve without leaving clear marks in the snow. There was also the evidence of Miss Harman, which brings the time forward to quarter past twelve. As to Miss Harman's evidence which was so critical and which disturbed the police so much, I'm copying certain passages below:

'This face at the window, can't you describe it in more detail?'

'No. It was horrible: deathly pale, with coarse features.'

'He was wearing a hat, wasn't he? You told us that the shadow which fled as soon as you saw it was wearing –.'

'Yes, I'm sure of it, but when he had his face pressed against the window, it was difficult to tell.'

'Are you quite sure that it was the same person who came back a quarter of an hour later?'

'I can't swear to it, but he did have the same look about him. Hat, long coat, furtive walk.'

'And you say he went in through the tower door without knocking?'

'Yes, I think so. You know, it's difficult to say, because he seemed to be hesitant. He was walking very slowly. And he could have knocked on the second door for all I know: the one leading directly to Edwin's room. And, besides, the first door leading from the courtyard was never locked.'

'Which seems to indicate someone who knows the lie of the land very well. Right. Next you told us there was a light in the room.'

'Yes.'

'And you saw shadows moving behind the window?'

'In fact, I couldn't really make anything out because the curtains were almost drawn.'

'And then you thought it might be a friend of Edwin's?'

'Well, yes, because there didn't seem to be any fighting.'

'Miss Harman, you told us that because of the full moon, it was almost as bright as day. Yet, when you describe Miss Mansfield's assailant, everything is vague.'

'That's because I had just woken up because of all those noises.'

'All those noises? That's pretty vague, too.'

'Muffled sounds, things falling over. I don't know. As I told you, I was asleep.'

'Let's get back to the shadow attacking Miss Mansfield.'

'I believe it was the same figure as before, but it all happened so fast I can't really be sure.'

'And how exactly did it attack Miss Mansfield?'

'It – They were fighting hand to hand, I believe. It's really difficult to say because I hardly had time to – I cried out, I opened the window and … there was only Miss Sibyl there.'

'And how long did it last?'

'Five seconds at most.'

'Maybe ten?'

'No, not that long. At least, I don't believe so.'

The police were obviously counting on Sibyl's testimony to learn more but they were disappointed because she is frequently subject to bouts of somnambulism, which was in fact the case that night. A state of affairs, I may add, which left them highly incredulous and

suspicious of her testimony. Here are Sibyl's replies during the
second interview with the inspector in charge of the enquiries:

'I repeat, Inspector, I was very tired, which happens often in such cases.'

'You definitely "came to your senses" when you heard the noise?'

'I think so. I remember the shrill cry of a woman.'

'And you didn't realise someone was attacking you?'

'Well, yes, I felt someone was holding me.'

'Someone was holding you? Could you be more precise?'

'I know someone was struggling with me and was trying to hold me down by force, squeezing me and making my arms hurt.'

'And when you opened your eyes you didn't see anyone? Not even a shadow?'

'No, I never saw any such thing. Please try to understand: I had just opened my eyes and it was dark. The first thing I saw was that blinding stream of light in front of the open door of the tower. It's not really surprising that I didn't see anyone running in the opposite direction and taking advantage of the darkness. In any case, I stood quite still but then… the scream. It came from Miss Harman, I believe … it paralysed me.'

'That was quite a bit of luck, because if you'd move three or four steps forward…'

What had happened? How did the assailant disappear so fast?
And without leaving any traces in the snow? Were Sibyl and Miss
Harman both suffering from delusions? The same vision at the same
moment… that would be too much of a coincidence, particularly since
Edwin had just been killed by a creature which left no trace on the
snow while fleeing.

Although the doctor found bruises on Sibyl's arms and shoulders
which appeared to have been caused by stronger hands than hers –
she also had marks on her face and a cut on her lower lip – the police
were inclined to believe her guilty. For, in the final analysis, she was
probably the only one who could have done it.

(At this point there was a description of the police officer's futile attempt to leap the gap, which Daphne had told me about, and which served only to demonstrate the absurdity of the police's suspicions about Sibyl.)

Piggott occupied the room next to the victim's. Having been
awakened suddenly, he ran to the door at the end of the corridor.
After having vainly tried the doorknob, he turned back, only to bump

*into Mansfield who was coming out of his room. They went to the
main entrance and then crossed the courtyard. They were the first on
the scene of the crime. Wisely, they touched nothing, each acting as
witness for the other. They had found Edwin in agony; he had
murmured a couple of words before expiring. They were scarcely
audible, but might have been "Lord" and "Misrule" although they
couldn't swear to it. What state was the room in? Corridor door
locked and windows secured from the inside. But read the words of a
young police officer who filed the following report:*

You would have thought the place had been struck by a cyclone.
The victim was lying on the carpet in the middle of the room. To his
left, a bookcase had been overturned with all its contents: books, little
pottery pieces, a bronze statue, an unopened bottle of port and some
glasses, mostly broken. The chimney is in the northern wall of the
room, far to the right of the door to the corridor and just to the right of
where the bookcase had been standing. But the poker, tongs, bellows
and fireguard were next to the body and the armchair in front of the
hearth had also been overturned; only the firedogs were in their right
place. The fire was almost out, but amongst the ashes were the
remains of a pullover and fragments of broken glass from a wine
bottle. The bed opposite the chimney was upside down and, where the
pillow should have been, there was a painting which had obviously
come from the wall overhead.

The canvas, which showed a naval battle, was slashed from top to
bottom. On the bedside table – between the bed and the east window
and therefore directly opposite the door opening onto the courtyard
via the tower – an oil lamp, which strangely had been left untouched,
illuminated the scene. The ceiling lamp was also lit. In the corner
diagonally opposite the chimney was a large wardrobe with its doors
shut, inside which were various clothes which also seemed to have
been spared, probably because the key seemed difficult to turn.

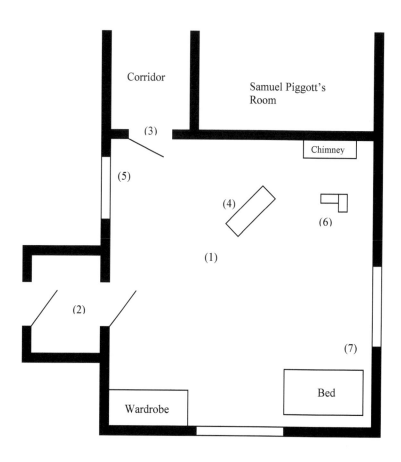

Corridor

Samuel Piggott's Room

(3)

(5)

Chimney

(4)

(6)

(1)

(2)

(7)

Bed

Wardrobe

EDWIN'S ROOM

(1) Where the body was found
(2) Tower, where both doors were
found open
(3) Door giving access to corridor
(locked on the inside)
(4) Overturned bookcase
(5) Window with half-drawn curtains
(6) Overturned armchair
(7) Bedside table

On the floor to the right of the bed was a half-empty bottle of whisky bearing traces of blood. The victim was lying on his stomach, his head towards the door leading to the courtyard and his features frozen in an expression of utter agony. He was wearing a waistcoat and trousers the same colour as the jacket – which was found on the bed between the covers – and a shirt whose sleeves were slashed and covered in blood. There were wounds on the back of his hands and a few faint streaks of blood on his face.'

The medical examiner was in no doubt as to the cause of death: two wounds in the abdomen, made with a long and extremely thin blade, had caused an internal haemorrhage. The victim did not die immediately and must have suffered a great deal. The superficial wounds to the arms and hands could have been inflicted by the same weapon, but those on the face were undoubtedly made by fingernails. The killer, in his murderous rage, had gone so far as to scratch his victim's face!

The weapon was never found, despite a painstaking search of the room, which thus excluded – as if that were necessary – the possibility of suicide or accident. No secret passage was found and the search also demonstrated the utter impossibility for the killer to have escaped by the windows – the classic guillotine type – for not only was the snow on and under the sills unbroken but the windows themselves were bolted from the inside. The bolt on the door connecting to the corridor was shot. Was Edwin in the habit of locking it when he returned to his room? The family and the staff believed not, but had never actually verified the fact. Be that as it may, it was an old and stiff bolt without any scratch marks and, according to the police, could not have been manipulated from the other side by any trick involving pins and string.

How had the tragedy unfolded and, above all, how had the murderer made his escape?

It wasn't the first question which bothered the investigators. The murderer was obviously the person Miss Harman had seen entering the tower door at quarter past twelve, and who must have been known to the victim, for why else would he have allowed him to stay so long and in such relatively calm circumstances, as Miss Harman had testified? It was after she went to bed that things must have taken a turn for the worse. There had clearly been a fight, as shown by the evidence, but possibly a silent one, as sometimes occurs when the adversaries are anxious above all to avoid attracting attention. Or perhaps everything happened very quickly. In any case, the murderer had to flee after the racket made by the bookcase overturning. As for the second question, one of the police officers suggested the possibility of acrobatics involving the wooden gallery above the courtyard. But that idea was swiftly discarded. For one thing, the thin coat of undisturbed dust on the floor proved that nobody had put a foot there for several weeks, and for another the access to the stairs within the tower were blocked to the point that not even a child could have got through.

The facts proved that no human being could have perpetrated the crime, nor even put a foot in the courtyard after twelve thirty. The police found no traces in the snow surrounding the house, apart from the footprints of those going for help. Which seemed to indicate that the murderer was among those present that night. But, in that case, why was he not subject to the laws of gravity like everyone else?

As for the motive for the murder, that also was a mystery for nobody knew of anyone harbouring a grudge against the cheerful Edwin. There remains the legend of the Lord of Misrule, that mysterious shadow with the deathly pale face who has haunted the premises for centuries and of whom you will have undoubtedly already heard by the time you read these lines.

12

FINAL PREPARATIONS

The following day, in the late morning, I helped my "fiancée" to negotiate the steps of the main entrance, full of attentive devotion and putting on a brave face for the benefit of the entire household, assembled to welcome us.

Her fragile arms made it difficult for her to move about on crutches, so that it was not long before she retired to her room to get some rest. I joined her shortly afterwards. Seated in a rocking-chair, her leg in plaster resting on a stool in front of her, she was gazing out of the window at the dazzling view of a landscape under an immense expanse of snow. But apparently the combination of sun and snow was not working its magic on her. The weak sigh she emitted upon seeing me confirmed as much.

'A beautiful day, isn't it?'

'Beautiful but glacial. One is better off closer to the fire,' I replied, rubbing my hands.

'You have to have been deprived of it to appreciate nature's true beauty,' she countered, with a feeble attempt at good cheer.

I went over to the window and pressed my forehead against the glass. A silver thread, starting at the corner of the stables behind the east wing, wound across the snow in the direction of the village. It was obviously the frozen stream I had crossed the other day with Daphne in my arms. I could still hear her peal of laughter as we tumbled in the snow, but I was quickly brought back to the present.

'You seem lost in thought, Mr. Stock.'

'Given the circumstances, that's hardly surprising. But first I must tell you that some of the people here, if not most of them, seem to be harbouring doubts about our relationship. I don't know whether we can pull the wool over their eyes much longer.'

It seemed to me that Catherine Piggott's expression saddened briefly, but she nodded her head slowly.

'Have you spoken to Edgar?' she asked.

'Yes, but only briefly. I got the impression he was quite surprised at your initiative: that's to say the idea of a fiancé-detective.'

Miss Piggott smiled mischievously.

'I know,' she simpered like a little girl. Then, looking modestly down, she added: 'You see, Edgar has quite taken a fancy to me.'

I was unable to hide my surprise.

'But – .'

'Quite. And you presumably wish to know whether the feeling is mutual?'

'Yes. Yes, that's it.'

'I believe so,' she said, somewhat embarrassed. 'But nobody knows yet, not even my brother. The fact that we've known each other for some time, and that we've never realized until – But that's of no interest to you,' she finished abruptly.

'Yes and no. It's best that I'm aware of the situation, if only with regard to Mr. Forbes.'

I went on to tell her about the events of the last forty-eight hours.

'Well, it seems you now know the whole story! Have you reached any conclusions?'

'Frankly speaking, no. On the other hand, it appears that the "detective" employed by you brother may be close to shedding some light on the matter, thanks to his powers....'

During the silence which followed, I looked at her out of the corner of my eye. Her expression did not reveal – as I had expected – her opinion of Julius Marganstone, nor did she offer any comment.

'In your opinion,' she asked suddenly, 'is my brother in trouble?'

'I don't think so. At least, no more than anyone else. But it's obvious that the "thing" which made an appearance at the Mansfield girls' windows does not bode well for the household.'

A few moments later I entered the dining room, which Daphne was in the process of decorating with silver-painted garlands, holly and mistletoe, not forgetting the yule tree standing proudly in one corner of the room.

I had forgotten that in a few hours we were going to be celebrating Christmas. The festive atmosphere which Daphne was trying to create was dampened somewhat by the presence of Sibyl and Piggott who, silent and sombre, were looking despondently out of the window. But for a brief glance they barely acknowledged my presence. As far as Sibyl was concerned, that was understandable – it was obviously best that we look at each other as little as possible. But Piggott? What did he think about me? Did he know that, at that moment, I would have given anything to hold his fiancée in my arms? The only thing I was sure of was that he was ill at ease. He was clearly worried about something.

I went over to join Daphne, who accepted my offer of help with enthusiasm. A quarter of an hour later, Mary came in to say Daphne was needed elsewhere. Her sister followed her, leaving me alone with Piggott. I approached Piggott – I could scarcely do otherwise – and after a few polite observations about the weather, he gave me his opinion about the séances presided over by his friend Morganstone. I replied cautiously that I found his powers astonishing, which didn't seem to satisfy him. After a strained silence, he asked me what I thought about the "Lord of Misrule."

Surprised, I stood there staring at him for several seconds. He had spoken without looking at me, apparently absorbed in contemplation of the sunset, but the concentration in his half-closed eyes betrayed him. With his left hand behind his back and his right playing with his golden watch chain, there was something proud and imposing about him which brought to mind a certain "little corporal." But the comparison stopped there, for it would be difficult to equate Piggott's commercial empire with that of the illustrious person who once dominated most of Europe.

'Difficult to say,' I replied, finally. 'Particularly since the legend goes back so many years. Let's see... Remind me of the name of that young fellow whose death started it all.'

'Peter Joke.'

'Ah, yes, Peter Joke. Well, I would say that if it isn't his ghost, then it's the ghost of one of the family members who swore vengeance on the Mansfields at the time.'

'Let me remind you, as you yourself pointed out, this business goes back a long time. Nearly two hundred years, in fact.'

'I'm well aware of that. And it's hard to believe that the recent tragedies were caused by ancient spirits. But there's nothing to stop one of Joke's descendants from taking up the cause. Are there, in fact, any members of the Joke family currently living in the vicinity?'

Piggott remained silent, so I continued:

'Well, I suppose not. Silly of me: that would have been the first thought in anyone's head.'

'You suppose wrongly, Mr. Stock. There is one living member of that family who cannot, alas, pass the name along.'

'A female, then?'

'A female whom you have met, in fact.'

'Living here?'

'Yes. Mary: the amiable and irreplaceable Mary. Joke was her maiden name and she's a direct descendant of the famous Peter Joke.'

I coughed into my hand to cover my embarrassment.

'Well, then, what I was saying is obviously stupid, for that charming woman is clearly above suspicion. She gets along admirably with Mr. Mansfield and his daughters and the legend – .'

' – a laughing matter,' interrupted Piggott. 'Or, rather, I should say *was*. For, over the last few years, since the famous white mask has reappeared and we've started to hear little bells tinkling again, nobody here has been laughing much.'

Indeed, as I had noticed myself, laughter was a rare commodity in this household. I could have counted the number of occurrences since my arrival on the fingers of one hand. And, to judge by Piggott's demeanour, the situation was unlikely to change in the coming minutes. His round face, with its greying sideboards, was looking increasingly worried.

'And, what's more,' I blurted out, seized by a sudden inspiration, 'Edwin's murder is at the heart of the matter.'

My observation shook him to the core. He turned towards me and stammered:

'D – do you really think so?'

'I do indeed. And I believe that once we've solved that crime, it will shine a light on everything else.'

'There are others who think that, too.'

'The thing that's strange about his murder, aside from the circumstances themselves, is the absence of motive. As far as I've been able to ascertain, Edwin was loved by all and sundry.'

'All and sundry? That's going, perhaps, a little too far.'

'Let me assure you that nobody has spoken a word against him.'

'Perhaps,' replied Piggott, with a curious smile. 'People rarely speak ill of the deceased. But I can tell you that he was not entirely the virtuous young man everyone has claimed. Oh, a charming enough fellow, full of good humour, a prankster even. All that's true. But did you know, for example that he was wooing his sister.'

'His sister?'

'His step-sister, to be exact. Sibyl.'

I stood there speechless.

'I find it quite deplorable and dishonourable, don't you, that he would attempt to profit from the second marriage of my dear friend.'

Who was he to speak of honour? And particularly on this subject! It was so grotesque that I controlled myself only with great difficulty.

'Sibyl never said a word, of course,' he continued. 'It was Charles, her father, who told me. Not that long ago, as a matter of fact. I can't say I was all that surprised, I must say, for I'd always found him a little odd and much too sure of himself. Anyway, Charles' confidence shed a blinding light on something which had appeared most curious to me at the time. You're aware, no doubt, that Sibyl had thrown her cap at that rather course young man you saw when you first arrived here?'

'A certain Harry Nichols, as I recall, who left suddenly one day.'

Piggott cleared his throat.

'Yes, yes. But he wasn't quite as uncouth as you may have been led to believe. In fact, he was the victim of a rather low trick. He'd been working for a friend of mine who ran a transportation company operating between Dover and Calais, and –.'

He stopped suddenly, gave me a sharp look, and shrugged his shoulders.

'But all that's of no importance,' he finished brusquely. All that's in the past. All you need to know is that the deceased was a man, just like the rest.'

To put it mildly, I thought. It had become clear that Piggott had not appreciated the charming Edwin, who had been killed in such a mysterious fashion. An idea was forming in my mind as I observed Piggott becoming more and more ill at ease in his starched collar and his tight-fitting waistcoat. Yes, that what it was: he was ill at ease. Ill at ease because a "spirit" had told *him* that *the explosive truth about Edwin's murder would soon be revealed.* If Piggott himself were the killer, one could readily understand why he had been less than thrilled to receive the message. Either someone was getting ready to blackmail him, or the Lord of Misrule himself was reminding him how little he appreciated being given credit for murders committed by others.

A RED CHRISTMAS

At midnight, the church bells rang out clearly and joyously in the bitter cold, their distant sound reaching us as the culmination of an emotional Christmas Eve. The mulled wine had warmed the atmosphere, had brought colour to the cheeks, had prompted shy smiles, and had loosened tongues. We welcomed warmly the traditional turkey and plum pudding prepared by the faithful Mary. Even the habitually mournful face of the lugubrious Julius Morganstone wore a smile; after a second glass of champagne he had announced that it would be pointless to attempt another séance that night. For the time being, I – and apparently the others, too – had forgotten the agonizing mystery that hung over our heads. Sibyl alone had seemed to remember, as she stole the occasional furtive glance at the windows. But there had been no reason for her to cry out in fear or in surprise. That night, the Lord of Misrule showed neither his dark silhouette nor his deathly white face; nor was there the slightest sound of tiny bells.

Did anyone think of him the following day, seated around the table enjoying the excellent Christmas feast of suckling pig? I doubt it. But after the meal, while I was congratulating the cook, there was again talk of the mysterious "spirit" and the message it had promised to transmit. A séance was to be arranged for that very evening, Julius Morganstone having announced that he sensed it would be fruitful. He had just made the announcement when Mary withdrew discreetly, having thanked me for my lavish – and well-deserved – compliments. I had turned my back to the table to speak to her, and as I watched her go I couldn't help thinking what a luck fellow Dudley was. As I turned back, I noticed out of the corner of my eye something remiss in the glass-fronted bookcase. Where the scintillating Spanish blade which I had so much admired had lain was an empty space.

Had it been taken for a purpose? Or had it simply been misplaced? And how long had it been gone? For a moment I considered investigating the matter, but then concluded it would be best to do nothing. My fears were no doubt groundless and would only serve to disrupt the happy proceedings.

The afternoon was given over to whist. My partner was Miss Piggott who turned out to be very skilful. Sibyl made several careless mistakes which her partner and fiancé forgave her with an obvious condescension. Daphne, who was partnered with her father, seemed to be enjoying herself despite his obvious lack of ability.

Night fell. After dinner, pleading a headache, I retired to my room to reflect about what had happened. I remembered Owen's words of the other evening: "The fact that *he* wants to speak to Piggott intrigues me enormously." He had laid heavy emphasis on those words. Owen had been quicker than I to envisage Piggott's involvement in Edwin's murder. But had he just been talking about the "spirit's" message or had he discovered something more in the dossier he had given me? I read through his notes once again, without finding anything in support of my suspicions, other than the fact that Piggott's room was adjacent to the victim's.

I looked at my watch: 9 o'clock. Another hour before Julius Morganstone would begin calling on the powers from the world beyond. I racked my brains without success about the best way to unmask the knocking spirit, then decided to rejoin Miss Piggott, paying a brief visit to the "Ladies' Workshop." What a charming title and how well it suited one of its occupants!

Sibyl was there, alone; still in the same spot, fragile, pale, and more desirable than ever. Never having known Edwin, I wasn't in a position to pass judgment on him but – supposing that what Piggott had said was true and he had been wooing Sibyl – I could hardly blame him. In his place, given the presence of a sister that really wasn't one, I would probably not have behaved any differently. Besides, in the present circumstances, it was not appropriate for me to take a moral position, given the intentions that had drawn me here.

As I entered, she raised her beautiful eyes under their long black lashes, giving me a look that was part invitation, part reproach.

I sat down beside her with a calm I was far from feeling and feigned interest in the lace mat she was embroidering.

'Has Miss Piggott already gone to bed?' she asked.

'No, I don't think so. She's still in the drawing room, as far as I know.'

'Ah!'

The message was clear. I changed the subject:

'Mr. Julius Morganstone is very hopeful about tonight's séance. Who knows, we may learn the truth about Edwin's mysterious end and even the name of his killer.'

'But we know who it is!' she exclaimed. 'It's *him*!'

'*Him?* The Lord of Misrule? But – .'

'But of course! Who else could it be?' she said, more hesitantly.

'Well, the "spirit" didn't seem to share that opinion,' I pointed out.

Sibyl's hands were trembling so much she had to put her work down.

'It's him, I tell you. Miss Harman saw him that night, didn't she? And the shadow and the white face we see every Christmas, who else do you think it could be?'

'It could just be a prankster.'

'A prankster who kills people?'

Her face became distorted. I tried to calm her down, but my words must have been badly chosen because she balked:

'But don't you understand? He'll be back soon to – to – .'

'Sibyl, I beg you....'

She stared at the window, motionless, and murmured:

'He'll be back soon....'

When I saw the tears spring to her eyes, I took her into my arms to try and stem the flood of tears I could sense was coming. Her whole body was trembling. With fear? Certainly, but of whom? The Lord of Misrule? Was she afraid for herself or for someone else? For Piggott? No, that wasn't possible. It must be that she was dreadfully sad at the prospect of her imminent marriage. Yes, that was it.

What precious moments those were, holding her pressed against me: the graceful, tearful fawn whose heartbeat slowed to match my own. Precious moments which, alas! did not last. She sat up suddenly and when I saw the distant, hard look on her face I knew it was over.

'I think it would be better if you left now,' she said, picking up her embroidery.

I obeyed in silence.

I saw her again at ten o'clock as we were all seated around the round table, including Catherine Piggott who, despite her injury, had joined us. We thus numbered ten, in clockwise order starting on my left: Miss Piggott, Nicholas, Mary, Charles Mansfield, Samuel Piggott, Sibyl, Morganstone, Forbes, Daphne and myself. They all seemed tense as they waited, Piggott more than anyone.

It was with difficulty that I observed my neighbours once the lamps were extinguished. The flames from the fire barely illuminated the faces and the hands placed on the table (which, I was able to verify, did indeed number twenty.) The rapidity of the "spirit's" appearance once Morganstone started his questions, and the vehemence with which it knocked on the table, startled everyone. The table shook so violently that it even rose slightly off the floor at the point where I was seated. It was quite incredible. A second occurrence was even more violent: the table seemed almost to lurch towards me and it was all I could do to hold it down, with the help of those adjacent to me.

It seemed inconceivable to me that anyone seated around the table could have caused it to move like that. It was not particularly heavy, but it was no ordinary pedestal table for all that: the feet were placed at its circumference, making it very difficult to tip over. And, as I've already explained, it didn't merely shake: it was almost as if it had been thrown at me. And all the while, every hand was still placed on its surface. Even someone seated opposite to me and pressing hard with a foot or a knee could not have caused such a displacement.

Our fingers were still touching as we all tried to dampen the violent shaking. Fear – nay, terror – was written to varying degrees on all the faces. There was no longer any doubt that we were in the presence of a real spirit and not a prankster, as some of us – myself included – had previously supposed. The calmest figure amongst us appeared to be Morganstone himself, although he, too, was perspiring. As for Edgar Forbes, normally a very composed individual, he was as white as a sheet and sat transfixed, his eyes bulging and his lips trembling with fear.

The "spirit" was the same as in the previous séances, communicating as before with one knock for "yes" and silence for "no." And it was still prepared to reveal the truth to Piggott.

'The truth... the whole truth?' asked Morganstone.

A single knock.

The medium looked around as if to ensure the participants' full attention.

'Very well. But when will you be ready to do so? Tomorrow?... Tonight?... Now?'

Another single knock.

'Now?' repeated the medium.

Yes.

'Now? You are ready to talk to Mr. Piggott?'

Yes.

'Here?'

No.

'Then where?'

Once again, it was necessary to use the alphabetic system, which yielded the letters:

A L O N E

'Ah, I understand. You wish to speak to Mr. Piggott and only to him?'

Yes.

'Where do you wish to speak to him, then?'

N O W and A L O N E

'You wish to speak to him immediately and only to him. So much is clear,' said Morganstone calmly. 'But you haven't told us where, precisely.'

B A R G E

'At the barge, is that correct?'

Yes.

Morganstone looked questioningly around the table. There was a momentary silence, broken by Charles Mansfield, who exclaimed:

'But, of course, the barge! By the lake. There's a barge down there.'

Morganstone asked for verification. The spirit replied three times in the affirmative, then fell silent. Once again the lamps were lit. Piggott tried in vain to conceal the fact that his hands were trembling.

'Do I have to go to the lake right now?' he stammered. 'But – but is it wise?'

Morganstone gave him a withering look and enquired solemnly:

'Why did you engage my services, Mr. Piggott?'

'Samuel, for our sakes,' begged Mansfield. 'Think of peace at last for our family. We're in your hands.'

For the first time since I had met him I felt almost sorry for Piggott. For, aside from Sibyl and her sister who appeared undecided, and Forbes who was totally confused, the others made it clear from their looks what they expected of him. Refusal on his part would have meant instant disgrace. I couldn't tell whether his obvious fear was that of a murderer facing exposure or that of an innocent man facing death. In either case, I wouldn't have wanted to be in his shoes. Yet, bewildered as I was by the events, I nevertheless remembered why I had been put there in the first place. It would be far too dangerous to allow Piggott to leave without at least a small escort, which is what I hastily proposed. A sort of rearguard, following far enough behind to avoid discovery, yet close enough to respond to a cry for help. Piggott's relief at the idea was palpable, particularly when Nicholas volunteered to accompany me.

No sooner said than done. Ten minutes later, wrapped up to the eyeballs, Piggott, Nicholas and I slipped out of the house via the servants' entrance. Daphne had tried to join us but her father had put his foot firmly down and in her annoyance she had gone to her room. Sibyl had burst into tears, but this time it was Mary that had taken her in her arms to comfort her. Morganstone had remained slumped in his chair, perspiring profusely as he always did after each séance. Edgar Forbes had vanished, but Catherine Piggott, sombre and silent, had accompanied us to the door.

The night was clear, but windy and cold. The snow-covered fields were bathed in the eerie light of the full moon, almost as revealing as daylight. The wind blew in gusts from east to west, bringing with it the occasional flurry of snowflakes and sweeping across the great white expanse which lay before us, smooth and utterly deserted.

Piggott turned round to make a sign with his hand, then set off in a determined fashion directly north.

We followed him in a leisurely manner until he was a hundred yards ahead, then quickened our step. Piggott was moving at a goodly pace. As his silhouette shrank in the distance, I asked my companion how far it was to the lake.

'A little less than a mile,' he replied. 'About a quarter of an hour in this snow. Can you see that little hill in the distance, over to your left?'

'Yes, I think I can make out something.'

'The lake is just behind there. But you'll see it soon enough.'

The further we got from the house, the stronger the wind blew. Even the snowflakes themselves seemed to fall more thickly, but it must have been a passing snowfall because the sky towards the east, where previously no star had been visible, seemed to be clearing. While I listened to the incessant crunching of our boots on the snow, I ran over and over in my mind the incredible events of the tragedy, over which hung the frightening shadow of the Lord of Misrule. Suddenly I had a premonition of imminent danger.

Over the last few days I had formed a picture of The Lord of Misrule in my mind: a deathly white mask of a face; a fluttering cape; the sound of tiny bells tinkling; an uncanny ability to float over the ground like a bird of prey and leave no prints. But now, with a sudden intensity, I felt his presence close to me. The moaning of the wind seemed like a bitter howl of resentment against his friends whose stupid games had led to his plunge into frozen waters. It was if I were listening to his last desperate cries for help as his hand began to slide into that black hole in the ice.

The distant figure of Piggott continued to advance steadily towards the lake....

The lake, which had been the scene of the tragedy nearly two hundred years ago; the lake which was *his* domain; which *he* came back to haunt every year at Christmas.

What we were doing was surely not reasonable. We should have called to Piggott to join us and the three of us should have turned about and gone back. I glanced at my companion whose eyes were glued to the clear footprints left by Piggott. I wanted to share my fears with him, but the grim determination in his face dissuaded me.

We had been walking for twenty minutes or so when we saw Piggott disappear over the brow of the hill we were about to climb. He was still about a hundred yards ahead of us. A few minutes later we reached the same spot which overlooked the lake, slightly to our right: an immense oval expanse of grey and white stretched out in front of us for about three hundred yards. To the east, straggling and irregular clusters of weeds marked the banks and in the distance we could just make out a skeletal group of trees. Ahead of us, the lake was unobstructed save for the little barge trapped in the ice not far from the bank, towards which Piggott was headed. For a distance of a hundred and fifty yards in either direction there was not a living soul – I swear it. The whole scene – with the exception of the occasional flurry of snow – was brilliantly illuminated by the full moon; every inch of the terrain was visible and it was obvious there could be not the slightest hiding-place for any human being.

At that point Piggott was perhaps twenty yards from the barge. To reach him from where we stood meant travelling down into a small depression and up over another mound. Nicholas pointed out that, if we did not wish to be seen, we should remain behind this mound which would serve as an excellent observation post.

It took us about a minute to get there, during which time we lost sight of Piggott. Despite the lugubrious moaning of the wind we could vaguely make out strange and distant sounds like a series of short hisses or whistles, which we were unable to identify. The choking cry we heard as we reached the bottom of the depression, on the other hand, left no doubt in our minds: it was clearly human and could only have come from Piggott. We looked at each other with dread in our hearts and hastened to the brow of the mound.

Standing there, I sensed something unreal about the frozen scene. The lake and its surrounds, bathed in the silvery light of the moon, lay before us in a deathly silence strangely underscored by the noise of the wind. Nothing had changed. Everything was still, including Piggott who was lying in the snow on the bank, just in front of the barge.

We hastened down the final slope, knowing in our hearts that it was futile. Piggott lay hunched on his right side, his right hand next to his bare head seeming to reach out for his nearby hat which, curiously, lay upside-down. The tip of his scarf was fluttering in the wind. His left hand was reaching towards his chest from which protruded, I had no doubt, the dagger which had disappeared from the bookcase earlier that day.

I had realised, immediately I had seen him lying there, that he had been murdered, but it was only now that the true nature of the situation began to dawn on me. Because what we were looking at defied all reason. The murder *simply could not have been committed.*

There were no traces of prints around the body. Nor were there any on the bank or the lake which, even though frozen, would surely have shown traces on the powdery snow if someone had trodden there. Nobody could have approached him from where we stood, nor from any other place on our journey, because we had not seen any prints but his in the snow. But that wasn't all. We had witnessed with our own eyes something even more bewildering: while Piggott was still alive, we had stood at the brow of the hill and observed, without a shadow of doubt, that there was no living creature within a hundred yards of him. And, less than a minute later, as he lay dead in front of the barge, the same statement was true. How, in the space of less than a minute, could any human being swoop on his victim, kill him, and disappear as miraculously as he had come? And without leaving the slightest trace?

Once more, blood had flowed at Christmas. The murderer had signed his name. The Lord of Misrule had been true to the legend. And the swirling flakes continued to dance over his frozen grave.

14

DEATH HAD WINGS

'The silhouette of a barge, resting peacefully on a lake against a wintry background. Is there anything more beautiful? No. There's too much poetry and purity in the composition to be anything other than the work of an artist, as I've been trying to tell you,' declared Owen Burns the next day as we stood – Burns, Wedekind and myself – under an overcast sky next to the spot where the outline of Piggott's corpse could still be seen.

Dispatched by Scotland Yard, at the request of the local constabulary, into whose lap the extraordinary crime had dropped in the middle of the night, Inspector Frank Wedekind had arrived practically at the same time as Owen, whom I had telegraphed early that very morning.

It turned out that the two men had met each other in the course of an investigation during which my friend had been called in by the Yard and solved the mystery in short order. Despite a pair of formidable eyebrows which gave him a stern look, Inspector Frank Wedekind, who appeared to be in his forties, seemed calm and level-headed. At least, as far as that was possible, for I doubted that any of his colleagues in the celebrated Metropolitan Police could have shown as much patience in the presence of my eccentric friend.

Owen had just picked up a handful of snow in his inevitably pale yellow gloves, saying:

'You must understand that I would never have acceded to Miss Piggott's request had not the case presented some unusual aspects. And I must say I did the right thing, for it has turned out to be quite remarkable, has it not? It was impossible for the murderer to have had the time to act; according to two reliable witnesses he left not a trace; yet the victim was found with a dagger through the heart which he could scarcely have put there himself. Superb! I must confess that my feelings about this murder are those I would feel towards a work of art.

'You seem to be forgetting the suicide theory,' observed Wedekind quietly.

'Suicide? Why that's quite absurd. Do you really think the victim would have come all this way in such trying conditions for the purpose of killing himself? It would be madness. Come now, admit it, it's hardly reasonable.'

'Reasonable or not, it's the only possible explanation. And the only one the coroner's likely to accept, however curious Piggott's behaviour might have been. It may turn out, during the course of the inquest, that Piggott had good reason to end his own life. Now, if we happened to turn up something to support the theory of a crime, that'd be another matter altogether.'

Wedekind stopped because Owen appeared not to be listening, seemingly occupied with the examination of the snow in his hand through a magnifying glass which he had produced from one of his pockets.

'A work of art. The design of the crystals. Such wonderful geometry....'

At the request of the inspector, I recounted the events which had followed our discovery of the body:

'After deciding there was absolutely nothing we could do for Piggott, Nicholas and I retraced our steps and it was just before we arrived back at the house that we saw him. I didn't recognise him at first. Neither did Nicholas for that matter. He was zig-zagging through the snow like a drunkard and uttering incomprehensible noises which sounded almost like cries of distress. We had no trouble catching up with him and it was only then that we recognized the haggard features of Edgar Forbes beneath the peak of his hunting cap. He was quite clearly not his normal self and seemed to have had some sort of demonic encounter from which he had been fleeing for several miles. He was completely out of breath, gulping in the cold air and expelling it in great clouds of steam like a locomotive. "I saw him," he said between gasps. "I saw him floating over the snow. He wanted to kill me, there's no doubt about it. I ran and ran. Be careful, he can't be far away." He continued babbling the same inanities as we escorted him back to the house. Then we left together to alert the police.'

'That's someone we should talk to right away,' declared the inspector as a policeman came hurriedly towards us. 'Have you found something, Kelly?'

The policeman stopped to catch his breath and shot a brief look at the three of us.

'Yes and no,' he replied grimly. 'We managed to trace the path followed by this Forbes fellow.' He thought for a moment, then went down on one knee in order to trace a circle in the snow. 'Here's the house.' He drew another circle to the north of the first. 'Here's the lake.' Connecting the two circles with a line, he continued: 'There's a gentle upward slope starting from the house resulting in the small hill just behind us. The victim's trail went to the left of this line: in other words, to the west. Forbes' trail went to the east. We were able to follow his trail: there were no prints other than his own and they left from the service entrance. Outward bound, he wasn't running, but he kept up a good pace. He had travelled just under a mile – in other words two-thirds of the way to the lake – when suddenly he turned round and started to run. Initially he ran in a straight line for two or three hundred yards, but then he started to zigzag as if he'd lost his senses, but still headed in the direction of the house. At that point, his prints became intermingled with those of the two witnesses who came back from the lake.'

'So he never got as far as the lake?'

'No. As far as we can tell, he couldn't have done. For a time we thought so because his prints crossed the little stream that flows from the lake.' He drew another line, to the right of the first. 'Here's the stream. He crossed it at about the half-way point as he was making his way back. Our first thought was that he could have doubled back upstream to the lake, but in fact that's almost impossible. He would have had to have been extraordinarily careful, not to mention extremely luckily, not to have broken the ice over the little trickle of water. And, in any case, Forbes left a very clear trail. Speaking of ice....'

He turned to look thoughtfully in the direction of the lake, and continued:

'The lake isn't as frozen over as it looks. Only the edges are navigable, so to speak. Even there, at certain spots, it can be dangerous. Fred got his feet wet there just a moment ago. You might say that's not surprising, given his weight. But Richard's built like a jockey and he went under. He was only three or four yards out from the bank when the ice gave way.'

'So, in other words nobody could have come from that direction?'

'Just possibly by following close to the bank, but only by moving very carefully, that's for sure. In any case, we didn't see any footprints on the surface of the lake, not that that means very much. With all that wind gusting over the powdery snow, any trace has probably gone already. Yes, did you want to say something, sir?'

The question was addressed to Owen .

'I just thought of something,' he said. 'If this stream draws water from the lake, I assume there's another somewhere that fills it up, so to speak.'

'Quite correct, sir, if I've understood your question properly.' He turned and pointed to a spot on the north bank of the lake. 'It enters over there and probably comes from the hill you can see in the background. But it's just the same as with the other stream: no broken ice. At least, as far as we went, because we didn't go back all the way to the source.'

'And around the lake?' asked the inspector.

'Nothing. No tracks at all, except those of a rabbit, near some trees. We also examined the three sets of footprints left by the victim and the chaps that followed him. They're very distinctive. As opposed to the tracks left by our men later, these are covered by a thin layer of powdery snow because it was still snowing slightly at the time of the crime.'

'Right,' cut in Wedekind. 'To sum it all up, Kelly, nobody other than the two witnesses could have got near the victim?'

'Correct. Nobody in the conditions as described. Of course, someone moving very slowly wearing very large snow-shoes might have left tracks which got covered with that last light sprinkle of snow, in which case we might have missed them. Or someone could have walked very carefully or even crawled along the frozen stream and the banks of the lakes, and so on. But there's the time constraint, isn't there?'

A few minutes later Owen, the inspector and I were looking at the lake from the brow of the hill. There was something sinister about the grey expanse of frozen water which was not entirely due to the leaden sky, nor the twisted trees in the distance, nor the reeds bowing under the repeated assaults of the wind. The lake and the two streams feeding and draining it were delineated against the unblemished white background of the fields by the reeds; rather more straggly to the north; rather more lush by the stream that descended towards the village. A sinister past had left its mark on this desolate spot: a baleful aura now revived again.

I had just walked, for the second time, from the hill down through the depression to reach the second mound, taking care to travel at the same speed as the previous night.

'Sixty seconds maximum,' declared Wedekind. 'You took all of a minute, during which time Piggott, hidden from your view, managed to get himself murdered. Now, look around. You told us there was no-one within at least a hundred yards of Piggott the last time you saw him alive, when he was approaching the barge. And there was nobody there a minute later when you saw him lying on the ground next to the barge?'

'Right. It was a full moon. It wasn't as bright as broad daylight, but I stand by what I said. And Mr. Dudley will confirm it, I feel sure.'

'If all this had happened in the summer, someone reasonably athletic could have done it. Run a hundred yards, strike the victim, and run back. No trouble. But on snow or ice, it seems it would be much more difficult, if not impossible. And after hearing my sergeant's report, I have to say worse than impossible! Even if you'd lost sight of the victim for two, three or four minutes.'

Owen nodded his head in agreement then, without looking at me, asked:

'And you claim to have heard hissing or whistling sounds, Achilles, during the time Piggott was out of sight. What kind of whistling? A flute? A bird? A steam engine?'

'Nothing of that kind. It was a faraway noise, I told you, scarcely audible. It seemed as if it was short and repeated. Maybe whistling is the wrong word. I really can't describe it any better.'

This time my friend looked at me, rather reproachfully I must say. After examining stretches of the bank at length – in vain, it appeared, despite the meaningful silences and mysterious airs – we repaired to the local inn, where several police officers, their cheeks red from the cold, were tucking into a simple but copious meal.

'This bacon is delicious,' observed Owen a little later. 'I wonder if it's the local air that gives it that aroma.'

'More likely several hours of exercise,' I replied.

'Very droll, Achilles. Now let's get down to business. Tell me all there is to know about the last forty-eight hours in the Mansfield residence. And don't forget to cover the events of last night.'

Disbelief was written on Wedekind's face as I finished my narrative; a narrative rich in detail, although silent on the matter of my feelings for Sibyl – luckily, as will be seen later.

'The only thing we can be sure of,' he said, passing round a box of small cigars, 'is the hour of death. The medical examiner is certain that Piggott died immediately after being stabbed, which puts it at 11 o'clock because you, Mr. Stock, and the coachman left the house at about 10.40 and you walked for about twenty minutes.'

'Twenty minutes is also the amount of time the murderer had to act,' observed Owen, lighting a match.

'So you're still sure it was murder?' asked Wedekind.

'But of course, Inspector. You're not about to tell me you believe in spirits, surely. The "message" which arranged a rendezvous with

Piggott by the lake was obviously a trap planned since the first séance. The table was obviously manipulated by the murderer.'

'But how?' I exclaimed. 'How, Owen, tell me? I'll swear it wasn't humanly possible.'

'Don't worry about the details. We'll talk about it after I've had a chance to look at the table.'

'I think Mr. Burns is right, at least on the last point. There must be a trick. But that doesn't mean it wasn't a suicide. I'd even go so far as to say it corroborates the supposition because Mr. Piggott was one of those at the séance. What could be more natural, given his bizarre behaviour up to that point, that it was he who made the table "speak"? A madman can be expected to act insanely.'

'Excellent, Inspector, excellent,' murmured Owen thoughtfully as he watched the smoke curling from his cigar. 'I'm speaking of your last observation, of course.'

The policeman smiled.

'Mind you, if you absolutely insist it was murder, there is a solution. Quite a simple one, in fact: the two fellows who discovered the body were in collusion. Don't worry, Mr. Stock, I'm not seriously considering it. You have nothing to be alarmed about, assuming the death doesn't affect you one way or the other.'

As I thought about Sibyl, liberated by the death of her fiancé, I realized from the look Owen gave me that he was ahead of me. He observed pointedly:

'Now listen here, Inspector, don't tell me you're going to take that tack in order to prevent my colleague and myself from finding the truth?'

'The truth? But that's all I'm interested in,' observed the policeman with the suspicion of a smile.

'Well, start by getting the idea of suicide out of your head. You must realise that this death, coming as it did at Christmas, can't just be another coincidence. This murder is undeniably connected to that of Mansfield's stepson, to last year's death and to those of earlier years. And don't forget that the lake is the Lord of Misrule's private hunting ground.'

'The Lord of Misrule,' echoed Wedekind, rolling his eyes. 'Don't tell me you believe in spirits now.'

'Not necessarily. But what I am saying is there's a connection between all these unfortunate events.'

Owen proceeded to list them all, to the growing consternation of the Scotland Yard man.

'It's incredible,' he muttered. 'I thought we'd concluded that Piggott could only have been killed by supernatural means. Murder? That would be truly incredible.'

'The more something is incredible, the more I'm inclined to believe it,' observed Owen pompously. 'For the time being, I propose we concentrate on the question of motive. Who would benefit from the death of Piggott? Or who could want him dead? Quite a few people, I would imagine. The first question is: who inherits his fortune? Without waiting for the will to be read, I would assume his sister must be a principal beneficiary.'

'Catherine Piggott?' I exclaimed. 'You think she might be the one even though it was she who first came to you because she feared for her brother's life? Why would she engage a detective to investigate a murder she herself was planning to commit?'

Owen looked at me disdainfully:

'What better way to divert attention?'

'And what do you make of her having her leg in plaster?' demanded Wedekind. 'A hopping murderer, that'd be something to write home about.'

'She would need an accomplice, that's all. Now, moving on to Forbes – .'

I interrupted my friend to remind him of the confidences Miss Piggott had made regarding Forbes' sentiments towards her. Owen drew triumphantly on his cigar and looked at the inspector:

'You see? Another suspect, and a prize one at that. If you'd seen Miss Piggott, Inspector, you'd realise it's unlikely he was in love with her just for her beautiful eyes. A golden goose, upon my word, and one ripe for the plucking I don't doubt. I find the recent blossoming of his feelings for her extremely suspect.'

The inspector looked thoughtful.

'Yes, I'd like to question that one. And I'd also be curious to know why he was wandering about at night and what he saw.'

'So would I, believe me. But let's not forget the others. As far as Julius Marganstone is concerned I can't see, off the top of my head, why he would be motivated to get rid of the person who hired him, but let's wait until we've interviewed him. For the Mansfields it's catastrophic from a financial point of view. From the human viewpoint, on the other hand – but let's listen to what you have to say, Achilles, for you're best equipped to talk about it.'

'As far as Sibyl and Daphne are concerned, I can assure you he was not dear to their hearts. Particularly the one that was betrothed to him. I'm quite convinced the marriage was a purely financial arrangement between Piggott and Mansfield. Sibyl had simply been sacrificed on the family altar. I'm convinced that she herself is quite incapable of killing a living thing, but I wouldn't be altogether surprised if she had subconsciously wished for Piggott's demise.'

'I'm beginning to get the picture,' said Wedekind, stroking his chin. 'There's no lack of motive, in fact. Apart from that, are there any others with a reason to hate him?'

'At least one,' said a new voice. It was the innkeeper, who must have been lending as ear to our discussion. 'And with a vengeance: Harry Nichols.'

15

WEDEKIND INVESTIGATES

As the innkeeper went off to attend to other patrons, we sat looking at each other in silence, his words still ringing in our ears: "'e's changed since 'e's been back. 'e used to be the life and soul. But these last few days 'e's like a bear wiv a sore 'ead. 'e sits 'ere all day wivout saying a dicky bird. But after 'e's 'ad a few, 'e starts running Piggott down a treat. Calls him all the names under the sun. I wouldn't repeat some of the things 'e says. It ain't pretty."

'Hell's bells,' Owen exclaimed, banging his fist in his palm. 'I remember now. I spoke to the boy the other day while I was waiting for you, Achilles. He was indeed rather uncomplimentary about Piggott at the time, but I wasn't really paying attention.'

I reminded my companions that I had seen Harry roaming around outside the house the day I arrived and I told them of my strange discussion with Piggott on Christmas Eve.

'All is still far from being clear,' declared Owen, 'but the truth is slowly starting to dawn. It would seem that Piggott – who already had designs on Sibyl – made arrangements with friends of his who owned the transportation company where Harry Nichols worked, to send him away and thus leave the field clear for himself.'

'I think a little chat with that young man is in order, said Wedekind, getting up. 'But first we have to hear what the Mansfields and their guests have to say.

Charles Mansfield made the drawing room available to us for the interviews, of which his was the first. On my return from the lake to inform him of the death of his friend, I had explained to him the true purpose of my stay. He hadn't held it against me, nor against Miss Piggott with whom he shared the profoundest regret at their loss. Indeed, the man seemed deeply affected by Piggott's death. He seemed to have shrunk suddenly and there was a desperate look in his eye. The inspector's first questions covered the actions of each of the residents, from the moment Piggott and his escort left, to the return of the latter. He himself had stayed a few minutes with Miss Piggott who had become anxious and excused herself, preferring to await her brother's return in her own room. He had noted the time: 10.45 and gone into the drawing room where Morganstone was recuperating from his exertions, as he hid after every séance. He had then retired to his study, where he had attempted to write a letter to a friend, but the agony of the wait had proved too much and he had not managed to write a single line. Daphne and Sibyl had gone to their rooms while Mary, it had seemed to him, had stayed a while with his elder daughter who had had a premonition of disaster. As for Forbes, he had only seen him on the occasion of our return, bringing the terrible news. At that time, it was about 11.30.

'So, Mr. Mansfield,' said Wedekind gently, 'you were very optimistic before your friend's departure. You thought that, after his rendezvous at the barge, he would return with information which would clear up many of the mysteries surrounding this house, didn't you?'

'Yes, I thought so. I did sincerely believe it. But he, on the other hand, was afraid of something. I had even felt it necessary to insist that he go as a matter of honour for his family and for ours. But, in fact, I simply sent him to his death.'

'So the "spirit" at the table lied to you?'

Charles Mansfield raised a pair of sad, weary eyes:

'It was a demon who communicated with us. *The* demon. *Our* demon, who comes every Christmas to take one of us. Well, he certainly managed to deceive us this time.'

'As I understand it, that's exactly what Samuel Piggott was afraid of and that's why he went to Mr. Morganstone.'

'Exactly. And we were counting on him. I'm not disputing his competence, but he was up against an adversary who was too strong.'

Wedekind got up to take a bag from a policeman who had just brought it in, opened it, and pulled out the dagger with the finely-worked handle.

'Do you recognise this, sir?' he asked.

'Of course. It belonged to my father, who claimed it came from a Spanish Armada wreck.'

'And where is it kept normally?'

Mansfield turned towards the bookcase next to the chimney:

'Behind the glass front, on the middle shelf, I think.'

'Did you notice it wasn't there?'

'No, but why are you asking?'

'Because this is the weapon which killed your friend. We know it wasn't there on the night before Christmas, but it was still there in the early evening.'

'Why are you telling me this?'

'Because I don't really believe in your "demon." I believe it was a human hand that took the weapon, with malice aforethought.'

Mansfield appeared perplexed.

'But I was led to believe that no human had –.'

'Quite true. In fact we believe that your friend did himself in, and he's actually the killer spirit.'

'But that's ridiculous.'

'So, according to you, he would have had no reason to kill himself?'

'None, other than a sudden brainstorm. Think about it: he brings in one of the topmost mediums in the land, fools him by simulating the presence of an evil spirit, and then arranges a meeting by the lake at which he kills himself. It makes no sense.'

'Particularly since he had every reason to look forward to next year,' added Owen.

'Quite right! He was to marry Sibyl at the end of the winter.'

'Which had been his fervent desire for some time?'

'Yes, indeed.'

Owen next spoke to him about Harry Nichols and what we knew of the affair.

Charles Mansfield seemed embarrassed.

'What has that to do with the recent events? In answer to your question, I don't know anything. As for me, I can't imagine Piggott stooping so low to get rid of Sibyl's ex-suitor.
But why don't you ask the fellow yourself, since he seems only too willing to talk about it?'

'We intend to do so. How did your daughter view the marriage?'

With a deep sigh, Mansfield replied:

'Well, I think she approached it in a very mature fashion.'

At which point, the inspector thanked the master of the house and asked that he send in Forbes. That gentleman, while not quite the frightened animal of the night before, was still far from regaining his normal calm assurance.

'Why did I go out?' he replied in answer to the inspector's question. 'Why, to protect my friend of course. I felt sure he was in danger and subsequent events proved I was right.'

'So you didn't believe in the "spirit" and his message of "truth"?'

Forbes turned crimson:

'No. At least not at the end.'

'Very well. Now tell us what happened when you went outside.'

He shrugged his shoulders:

'I'm not really sure. The more I think about it, the more it seems like a dream. I left the house five minutes after the others, so I was hurrying to catch up. My head was full of the sinister legends of the past, and I sensed imminent danger. After I'd been walking for a while, I suddenly heard a faint noise in the distance which appeared to be approaching rapidly.'

'A noise? What kind of a noise?'

'Very difficult to say. Perhaps like someone sawing. And then I suddenly saw a shadow emerge, moving at high speed above the snow. It was a black shape, but I couldn't tell you more than that. At the time, I was sure it was the Lord of Misrule, so I turned tail and ran as fast as I could. I've never run so fast in my life.'

'Do you think you might have been the victim of your own imagination?'

Forbes shrugged his shoulders again.

'Quite possibly. But it wouldn't be the first time strange things have happened in these parts.'

The inspector thought for a moment.

'In one sense, it's lucky you didn't reach Mr. Piggott.'

'What do you mean?' asked Forbes, his face now ashen.

'You know perfectly well what I mean. You could have been accused of murder.'

'Murder? But I'd heard it was impossible.'

'Tell me, Mr. Forbes, what is your professional standing at the present time? You were a partner of Mr. Piggott, were you not?'

'Partner? I was one of his employees. A senior position, I'll grant you, but – .'

'So his death didn't benefit you in any way?'

'Surely not. Quite the contrary. I risk losing a good position, if –.'

'If what?'

'If the company is sold.'

'Do you know the provisions of the deceased's will?'

'No, but I would imagine Miss Piggott would be the logical beneficiary.'

'From what I've heard, there may be a romantic attachment between the two of you.'

Edgar Forbes mumbled that it was a recent turn of events. The inspector changed the subject to the murder weapon, but with no more success than with Mansfield. Forbes recognised it immediately but had not noticed its disappearance. Owen took over to question him about Harry Nichols.

'I don't know anything,' replied Forbes, obviously ill at ease. 'I hardly even know the young man.'

'Oh? I thought I saw you with him the other day at the pub.'

'I'd gone there for a drink. He was there and we exchanged pleasantries. That's all.'

Edgar Forbes was thanked in his turn. As soon as he had left, Wedekind observed that he didn't seem to have a clear conscience.

'He was shaking with fear, more like it,' replied Owen who had taken out his magnifying glass and was preparing to examine the round table.

'What do you think of his story?'

'It was mostly for show. Although it's quite understandable that he was worried about Piggott.'

'I'm talking about the mysterious shadow he saw.'

'I don't know why you think that's important, given that you believe it was suicide. Achilles, this was the table used in the séance, wasn't it? My word, how light it is!'

'I never said otherwise. But try to lift it off the ground when your hands are flat on the table.'

'Come over here. The three of us will sit round the table and act as if we wanted to invoke the spirits.'

Owen proceeded to try a series of experiments while seated straight, his fingers spread out on the surface of the table. He varied the position of his feet and knees and the pressure of his hands without obtaining any tangible results. Then he asked us to step back while he subjected the table to a meticulous examination. For a brief moment I saw the flicker of a smile on his lips, but he said nothing as he stood up.

Mary came in after Forbes. She hadn't noticed the disappearance of the dagger either and her testimony only served to confirm that of Charles Mansfield. She had indeed accompanied Sibyl to her room and stayed with her for several minutes before returning to the kitchen to prepare breakfast for the following morning. Asked about possible reasons for Piggott's suicide, she retorted sharply that he wasn't the type. The way in which she spoke of the deceased, in polite platitudes, made it clear that she had had little sympathy for him. She was not overcome with grief, to say the least.

A very sad Catherine Piggott followed Mary. From 22.45 to 23.30 she had languished in her room, nursing the growing certainty that her brother was in great danger. To be frank about it, the tragic news hadn't come as a surprise. After all, hadn't events turned out exactly as she's expected? Hadn't she come to Owen Burns for help in the first place? It was out of the question that he brother had taken his own life. His business was prospering and he was full of anticipation for the coming year. She didn't know the details of her brother's will, but who other than she would naturally inherit? Sibyl?

It would be reasonable for him to have left her something, but she was sure he hadn't been in touch with his solicitor lately.

When came to Sibyl's turn, we were all shocked by the sickly pallor of her skin and the vacant stare in her eyes. She turned out to be of no help to us. As far as she was concerned, the house was haunted by a spirit against whom all resistance was futile. It was hard to discern any emotional feeling in what she was saying. All one could say with certainty was that she didn't resemble the grief-stricken fiancée she was supposed to be. I couldn't help noticing that Owen had clearly been struck by her beauty; I would have been surprised if he hadn't.

Daphne's testimony was as unhelpful as her sister's. She was at pains to remind me that I'd taken her father's side when he'd refused to let her accompany Nicholas and myself. She was convinced that, had she come along, her superior powers of observation could have saved Piggott. Owen could barely contain his mirth. I suspected he had been captivated by her personality. He thanked her warmly for her enlightening observations, complimented her on her beautiful ring, and hinted he would make use of her perspicacity during the rest of the investigation. She left blushing with pride.

'I didn't leave my chair the whole time,' declared Julius Morganstone warily after Wedekind asked him to account for his time during the hour following Piggott's departure.

'And you stayed there, in the dark, the whole time?'

'Yes, that's normally how long it takes me to recover the energy lost during a typical séance.'

'And this was a typical séance, would you say?'

Morganstone wrung his hands.

'Not exactly. It's the first time I've ever seen such a malevolent spirit.'

Wedekind continued scathingly:

'Speaking of spirits, I find the one you called up acted rather strangely. In the guise of speaking the truth, he makes an appointment with your client who is then found stabbed through the heart. How do you explain that?'

'But I don't explain it. My role is simply to set up contact with them. I'm not responsible for their acts.'

'You must be joking! You've sent a man – your own client – to his death and now you're washing your hands of the matter. That's too good to be true.'

Julius Morganstone stood up with an air of outraged dignity. His voice trembled with anger as he recited – by rank – a series of impressive regular clients who could attest to his integrity, making it clear he would make full use of his contacts to ruin the career of a certain Scotland Yard inspector, should he continue to treat him like a vulgar charlatan.

Ever prudent, Wedekind softened his tone.

'I fear I may not have expressed myself clearly. I wished merely to ask you your professional advice about the result – quite surprising, as I think you'll agree – of your last experiment.'

During the next half hour, Morganstone recapitulated the content of the various séances, of which I have already given the detail and will therefore not repeat. The inspector asked him under what circumstances Piggott had contacted him and what exactly he expected of him.

'I am not altogether unknown in the profession, Inspector, as you may have noticed,' the medium replied, once more wrapping himself in the cloak of dignity. 'He had realised I was the only one who could help him and so, quite naturally, he came to see me in my chambers about a month ago, to describe the case of the mysterious curse on the house of Mansfield. He made it clear he was about to marry into the family.'

'The matter of his own fate being more important to him than clearing up the mystery?'

'I believe so. But I made it clear to him that his own well-being was inevitably tied to the latter. We failed, I admit, and in a tragic manner. Furthermore, we haven't advanced an inch, even though I had high hopes at one point.'

Morganstone fell silent for a moment, then pointing a trembling finger at the detective, continued in a solemn voice:

'One thing is certain: the spirit that haunts this place is particularly malevolent and vindictive. He has extraordinary power and I confess never having encountered his equal in my entire career.'

16

ARIADNE'S THREAD

It was after five o'clock by the time we finally finished our interview with Julius Morganstone. Wedekind suggested that Owen accompany him to the village to seek out Harry Nichols, but Owen pointed out he wasn't really needed and would prefer to remain in the house with me to clear up some unfinished business. We agreed to meet later that evening in the inn where Owen had a room.

Once the inspector had left, Owen asked the master of the house for permission to take a look at what had once been Edwin's room. Charles Mansfield raised no objection and told us we would find it unchanged. He had made the decision, upon the death of the boy he considered to be practically his own son, to leave it as it was in memory of him.

He handed us the key and left us in the middle of the courtyard. We stopped to look up at the wooden gallery which made a dark bar across the grey winter sky. More than thirty feet long, it spanned the courtyard and connected the two towers at a height of some twenty feet above the ground.

'Do you think there's any connection between the gallery and the miraculous disappearance of Edwin's killer?' I asked.

Owen seemed amused by the question.

'You read the notes I gave you, I take it? Tell me, Achilles, do you know how best to find your way out of a labyrinth?

'Well, you take a thread –.'

'No, you're not starting from the entrance. You're in the middle, where you may even have been led with your eyes blindfolded. You're at the heart of an inextricably entangled jumble of paths, only one of which leads to daylight. In fact, it's where we now find ourselves, with this extraordinary legend which we somehow have to demystify. We haven't had the luxury of following the affair from the beginning and analysing each phase of its evolution. That would have been too simple. Instead, we were catapulted into a dark recess as far from the light as possible.'

'Enough of the poetic asides. How do we get out of here?'

'It's quite simple. Keep your right hand touching the wall at all times and advance slowly. You will inevitably reach the exit, even if you've had to cover every inch of the labyrinth.'

'Doesn't it work with the left hand as well?'

'Very good, Achilles. You've responded the way most women do, only slightly quicker. The point I was trying to make is that, after methodically running into every *cul-de-sac*, following each interminable corridor to its end, and exploring every path leading nowhere, we must inevitably discover the truth.'

'In other words it's just a question of method and time.'

Owen carefully adjusted his silk tie.

'For ordinary mortals of average intelligence, yes. But for the aesthete, there are other methods more subtle and more rapid. Come, let's not waste any more time.'

Moments later, we were in Edwin's cold, damp room. It was obvious the only care it had received had been an occasional dusting.

After lighting a lamp, Owen examined the lock on the door leading to the corridor, then the adjacent bookcase, and pulled a face.

'What a pity they didn't leave things as they were.'

'You mean as they were after the struggle?'

'Yes, but we couldn't really have expected it.'

He gave the rest of the room a cursory look, except for the wardrobe, whose contents he examined carefully before closing it. There was a faint smile, half-ironic, half-satisfied, on his lips.

'Achilles, do you know if Nicholas is here at the moment?'

'I think so, I thought I heard his horse just now.'

'Very good. Please ask him to come here.'

I complied without asking any questions and, shortly thereafter, Nicholas was in the room, seemingly as puzzled as I was.

'My dear Mr. Dudley,' declared Owen affably, designating the wardrobe which now stood open. 'Pray take a look inside.'

Nicholas' eyes bulged with surprise and indignation:

'But sir, those are poor Mr. Edwin's personal effects.'

'I know. But where's the harm? The police must have looked inside at the time.'

'Well, of course – .'

'But you didn't, did you?'

'No, why would I have done? Well, if you insist.'

Nicholas reluctantly sifted through a number of shirts as if he were committing a sacrilege. Reaching the jackets, he appeared to gain confidence when suddenly he stopped dead. He gave Owen a look of bewilderment as he pulled out a voluminous dark coat and examined it by the light of the lamp.

'I – It's – I do believe this is mine.'

'It does seem as though that article of clothing belongs to someone much bigger than the late Edwin, to judge by the rest of the items.'

'Yes,' murmured Nicholas. 'It's my greatcoat, the one that disappeared a while ago. But what's it doing here? It's unbelievable.'

'This wardrobe was a good hiding-place, was it not?'

The little clock in the "Ladies' Workshop" was striking six as I shared our discovery with Daphne and Sibyl. Owen – who had brought along a battered hat also found tucked away in Edward's wardrobe – seemed charmed by many of the objects in the room, and in particular an ancient spinning wheel. And he expressed a feigned rapture as he contemplated the woolly mittens Sibyl had knit.

'That's quite extraordinary,' said Daphne, with an admiring glance at Owen. 'We'd looked everywhere for it. How did you know it belonged to Nicholas?'

'Very simple. My friend had told me about its disappearance and I noticed it was considerably larger than anything else in the wardrobe. The conclusion was obvious.' His eyes wandered around the room. 'I say, this is by far the most beautiful room in the house. It's comfortable, peaceful, and furnished with an exquisite simplicity of taste, ideal for artistic inspiration. It's hardly surprising that it's here that your agile fingers make the adorable woollen creations I can see in the box over there.'

Sibyl blushed and smiled demurely. I felt a brief pang of jealousy towards my friend for having so effortlessly made the lovely Sibyl smile.

'Do you really find them pretty?' she asked.

'Very pretty. I can imagine how happy the children are when they put them on.'

'Which reminds me,' said Daphne, 'did you also find a cardigan in the wardrobe?'

'No, and it wasn't for want of looking, for I recalled that a cardigan had also disappeared at the same time. But tell me, did everything: wool, knitting needles and cardigan disappear, or was it just the cardigan ?'

Daphne shrugged her shoulders and turned to her sister, whose eyes clouded over.

'It seems such a long time ago,' said Sibyl after a long silence. 'There was nothing left on the bench, but... yes, I do believe that....'

She stood up and went over to the chest of drawers by the door, opened the topmost drawer and turned back to look at Owen, her face pallid.

'There were needles and balls of wool. Yes, I remember now, because I wouldn't have paid attention if they'd been in their normal place. As you can see, this drawer is reserved for embroidery. I found them several days after the tragedy, but... but.... '

Sibyl sat down again, deep in thought, then asked:

'Is that what you expected to here? Why did you ask me that?'

Owen continued to look at her as he adjusted his tie.

'You see, there are two aspects to art. On one side, there's the creation: the genius, the madness, the inspiration; and on the other, the cult of beauty: the love of perfection, the finish, the care, the attention to detail. As for me, I worship both categories, separately or — .'

'I'm afraid I don't follow you, Owen,' I interrupted. 'What does a ball of wool have to do with our mystery?'

'Ariadne's thread!' said Daphne.

'Remarkable!' exclaimed Owen. 'All one has to do to escape from the labyrinth is to follow the thread. Remarkable, isn't it Achilles? We were just talking about it. Young lady, may I make a further appeal to your perspicacity by asking if this hat suggests anything?'

Daphne's brow furled in concentration as she stared at the battered headgear. Then she looked at her sister, who said, after a moment:

'It seems to me that it belongs to Tim, our old gardener.

'Do you recall where he usually kept it?'

Sibyl rose to take it in her hands and examine it. Then she shook her head gracefully.

Owen persisted:

'Come now, don't you keep old articles of clothing like this in this very room?'

Sibyl looked at him for a moment, then turned to look at a wall cupboard as she nodded in the affirmative.

'In fact, there are a few old articles in there, now that I think about it. It's even likely that that old hat was kept there, but since it's been four years since old Tim died —.'

Just at that moment, there were three brief knocks on the door. It was Dudley, accompanied by a plain-clothes policeman who, breathlessly, his cheeks crimson from the cold, addressed Owen directly:

'The inspector wants you to join him immediately in the village. There's been another murder: a certain Harry Nichols.'

17

AND NOW, HARRY

The policeman led us towards the village at breakneck speed and ten minutes later we arrived exhausted at the stone bridge. Lantern lights could be seen moving below us along the river's edge. Two policemen were inspecting the snow-covered banks under the direction of a man in a bowler hat, who could only be Wedekind.

We went down to join him. Without a word, he led us to the base of the arch, where the snow was spattered with dark stains which we had no trouble identifying even before the lantern light illuminated them.

'They've just taken him away,' said the inspector solemnly. 'He's been stabbed in the back and wounded in the hand – almost certainly while trying to defend himself. It's that last wound which caused all the loss of blood you can see there.'

'Who found him?' asked Owen.

'I did, and quite a stroke of luck it was, too. He's not dead. He still has a chance of surviving. He's very weak, admittedly, but he's still hanging on.

'After I left you, I went looking for him at the pub. He wasn't there. Someone suggested I try his brother's house, not far from there. But when I got there, the brother told me Harry had left ten minutes ago, to go to the pub. I'd had a little trouble finding the house, so I hadn't followed the route Harry would've taken. I was getting frustrated because I seemed to be turning in circles. So I turned back, just as the clock struck 6.30. Luckily, it was just before I crossed the bridge, or else I probably wouldn't have heard the feeble moan. At first, I thought it was a cat, but even so I looked over the parapet and that's when I saw him, crouched like a hunting dog against the base of the arch, with his hand covered in blood and his face contorted with pain. There was a dark stain on his jacket as well, but no sign of the weapon. Even though he couldn't say anything, I immediately thought of Harry Nichols. Let's hope he pulls through.'

Still looking at the stains in the snow, Owen extracted a cigarette from its case and lit it calmly.

'So it must have been around 5.45 when he was attacked, and nobody saw it.'

'No. two of my men are questioning the locals, but so far without success.'

Owen looked around. Night had almost fallen, but the gloomy outlines of the houses on either side of the inn could still be seen, with their gables, their chimneys belching smoke, and the red splashes of their windows under snow-covered roofs.

'Not a fit night out for man or beast,' he sighed. Nor for looking out of the window, particularly since it started to get dark an hour ago. But what a risk the killer took. Look what might have happened – Look there, Inspector, there are two sets of tracks clearly visible in the snow. Probably those of Nichols and his assailant. Let's hope they haven't been too badly scuffed.'

'Don't get excited,' replied Wedekind calmly. 'I was able to examine the tracks before help came. The scene is very easy to reconstruct. The killer met Nichols as he was about to cross the bridge, lured him down here on some pretext, then took out his knife. Simple as that. As for the footprints, we've already taken the steps necessary to preserve them.'

'So,' I murmured, 'we're on the right track at last?'

Wedekind nodded.

'It'll be even better if Nichols recovers. Our man is at bay. He took a crazy risk attempting this murder, ignoring the most basic precautions. Clearly he must feel he's running out of time, which points to a motive: to ensure Nichols' silence before the police talked to him.'

'Excellent reasoning, Inspector,' said Owen approvingly. So now what's your plan of action?'

'I'm going to the hospital where they took Nichols to wait by his bedside, hoping he can give me the name of his assailant. For your part, you can return to the Mansfields.'

The new tragedy made the chill that already reigned over the Mansfield residence even colder, if that was possible. During the dinner, to which Owen had been invited, I attempted, between snippets of conversation, to determine each person's whereabouts at the critical time. The inspector had thought we stood a better chance of drawing out the information during casual conversation, before the official interrogation took place.

Owen and I had calculated that it would take a minimum of twenty minutes to go down to the village, commit the crime, and return. And even that assumed the good fortune of finding Nichols immediately on arrival. Who, then, could have absented themselves for twenty minutes prior to 5.45? Just about everyone, as it turned out, except Nicholas, whom I had taken to Edwin's room at about that time. It seemed highly unlikely that Sibyl and Daphne could have participated in that race against the clock, given that we found them sitting calmly in the "Ladies Workroom" at 6.00. Even less likely was Catherine Mansfield, with her foot still in plaster. That left Mansfield, Morganstone, and Forbes. The master of the house, who had been plunged into a sort of stupour by the death of his friend, seemed scarcely perturbed by this new attack. The other two, in contrast, were showing increased signs of nervousness. I watched them particularly closely when Owen repeated that we shouldn't lose hope because Inspector Wedekind could arrive at any moment to announce that Harry Nichols was going to pull through. I couldn't help thinking that, if one of them were indeed the guilty party, then he was a particularly rotten actor, because neither of them seemed the slightest bit pleased by the prospect. Mary, on the other hand, gave a fervent 'Pray God that he be saved.'

Mary. The good and faithful Mary, whom I had subconsciously eliminated from the list of suspects. She seemed the least likely person in the household to commit a reprehensible act of whatever kind. Which was precisely what attracted my attention at that moment. Whilst I was keeping a discreet eye on her, I recalled the time I had surprised her staring at the dagger in the glass-fronted bookcase, shortly before it disappearance. I remembered also my discussion with Piggott just before Christmas: 'You suppose wrongly, Mr. Stock,' he had said. 'There is one living member of that family... Mary: the amiable and irreplaceable Mary. Joke was her maiden name and she's a direct descendant of the famous Peter Joke.'

Was it possible that an evil spirit had instilled in her a desire for vengeance against the Mansfield family? That she was responsible for the four murders which had occurred over the last few years, not counting this last attack against Harry Nichols?

She was still a young woman and a pretty one: a veritable doll in comparison with her husband. Although small, she was very energetic. She appeared to everyone to be friendly, helpful and efficient. That was certain. But it had been apparent all along that her feelings towards Piggott were not of the warmest.

A little later, when Burns and I were able to snatch a few moments alone together in the kitchen, I shared my suspicions with him. He replied with a question:

'Have you watched the people walk?'

'Walk? Do you mean the way they walk?'

'Yes. The manner in which they place one foot in front of the other.'

'Why on earth would I do that?'

'Never mind. In any case, we've got him. I'm sure I'm right and I'll be able to expose him when it suits me. Meanwhile, I'd like you to go and find Sibyl and ask her to meet us in the "Ladies' Workshop." How I love that name! It suits her perfectly.'

We found her there, seated as usual in the superb high-backed chair which seemed to have been made for her, and more alluring than ever. I had the impression that, little by little, she was coming out of her shell and starting to live again, now that the sad prospect of her marriage to Piggott had been banished. I was dwelling on these beginnings of spring when Owen saw fit to evoke – apparently in all innocence – the memory of Harry Nichols. I cursed him under my breath.

As far as Sibyl was concerned, this latest attack could only be the work of "The Lord of Misrule." Her unshakeable belief in the existence of this sinister personage continued to astonish me. Whenever she spoke of him there seemed to be a determination in her voice which was normally absent. She did not consider his acts as vindictive recriminations, but rather she seemed to consider his presence in that place as a stroke of ill fortune, an inescapable stroke of bad luck, at least for the Mansfield family. From my perspective, I was certain that if Sibyl wanted to banish the nightmare from her life, she should leave the place once and for all, preferably with me alongside!

Time passed and the clock chimed each quarter of an hour in a quiet intimacy which embraced Owen, Sibyl and myself. She spoke slowly, at her own pace, but she spoke nevertheless and almost without a break, which had seldom been the case until now. She found, in Owen and myself, an attentive audience and one almost silent save for the occasional brief comment from my friend.

She spoke at length of her idyll with Harry Nichols. Did she still reserve a soft spot for him? No, except for the pity she felt for what had happened to him. But she acknowledged that his sudden disappearance had wounded her pride at the time. He had come to see her, incidentally, quite recently – in the last few days – to speak to her, to try to explain.

'Purely by chance – a lucky chance – it was I who opened the door. It was quite a shock to see him again. He told me he still loved me and it wasn't his fault that he'd had to leave so suddenly. In fact, it was Mr. Piggott's! I told him it would do him no good to speak ill of Mr. Piggott, for he was soon to become my husband. At which point he flew into a rage. He proceeded to tell me a host of bad things about

Samuel and I found it very difficult to get him to leave. Luckily there was nobody in the entrance hall at the time. If Samuel had been there, I shudder to think what might have happened.'

She stopped for a moment to count stitches, then continued:

'It pains me to say so, but I didn't love Samuel as I should have.'

It was only with a great effort that I contained myself.

'Papa always told me that it would come but by bit, once we were married.' She shrugged her shoulders. 'I'm sure he was right. In any case, Samuel was always very kind to me, bringing me little presents all the time. But there wasn't the same passion that there was with Harry, or with Edwin. Edwin always wanted to marry me, did you know? Edwin, my brother.' She smiled. 'He wasn't really my brother, of course, but all the same! And then there was Samuel.

'At first, I thought Edwin was teasing me, but I soon realized that what I had taken for an innocent joke hid some deep and very dangerous sentiments.'

As she was describing that short, clandestine idyll I was seized with a terrible jealousy. I sensed that, between Harry, Piggott and Edwin, it was the last whom she missed the most – and by far, even though she wouldn't admit it to herself.

Luckily, he was only here during the school holidays, because he became more and more forward each time he had the chance. I had thought my crush on Harry would annoy him. He gave me the cold shoulder for a while, but it didn't last. And after Harry left... And to think Papa knew nothing about any of it!'

'He would have been upset?' asked Owen.

'Of course. As far as he was concerned, even then, I was destined to marry Samuel. Yes, destined. In any case, there was no question of anything between Edwin and me.'

She stopped.

'Edwin,' she murmured plaintively, 'Edwin's gone, too.'

For a few seconds, we thought she would burst into tears, but then a curious and sudden metamorphosis took place, and the faraway look came back into her eyes.

'It's strange,' she said. 'Now that I think about it, all three of them, one after the other, have become victims of the Lord of Misrule.'

18

THE SPIRIT OF THE LAKE

It was one o'clock in the morning and I couldn't sleep. Snuggled under the blankets, I could hear the savage howling of the wind as I cast my mind back to the last talk with Owen, whom I had accompanied to the front entrance as he left to go back to the inn.

"The art of loosening tongues consists of knowing how to ask questions without opening one's mouth," he had lectured me. "Never forget that, Achilles. Silence is always the best way to make people to talk. I assume you realise that what we just heard from the mouth of the charming Sibyl is of paramount importance. And now, my friend, get a good night's sleep. You need to be in good shape tomorrow, for it's highly probable there will be an arrest."

I hadn't been able to learn more. He had already turned and started to walk away with long strides, to be quickly swallowed up in the shadows; for, in contrast to previous nights, this night was very black and heavy with snow.

I was forced to admit that, without apparent effort, he had indeed succeed in loosening Sibyl's tongue. Had it advanced the investigation? Owen seemed to think so. For my part, I was in a dense fog: a fog thick with mystery and about to get thicker....

An arrest tomorrow? But of whom? How could the way anyone walked mean anything? And what to make of the "reappearance" of Nicholas' coat? Or of a ball of wool? Or an old hat? What to make of "Ariadne's thread"?

Such unanswered questions danced around in my head until sleep finally overtook me. The last images I saw before losing consciousness were of a noisy and colourful procession led by the "Lord of Misrule" and his drunken acolytes, dancing in the streets and over the frozen lake.

The Lord of Misrule. The mysterious Lord of Misrule, who could travel across the snow without leaving a trace....

Outside, it had started to snow again and the wind was blowing harder and harder, to the point the windows were starting to rattle. Above the incessant moan, a new sound could be heard, a sort of tinkling noise....

Tinkling?

I sat bolt upright in the bed, fully alert, and stayed perfectly still for several seconds. I shivered from head to toe. I was not dreaming:

the sound I had heard and which was starting to fade away was, *without a shadow of doubt, a tinkling of tiny bells.*

With one bound, I was at the window.

The darkness and whirling snow severely reduced visibility and I probably would not have seen it if it had not moved. But it did move, slowly, towards the north, battling the snow. A dark silhouette – impossible to see anything clearly – which quickly disappeared from view.

With two murders in twenty-four hours, perpetrated in all likelihood by the figure I had just seen, it required a certain recklessness to follow it in the darkness. Yet that is what I did. Without a moment's hesitation.

Less than five minutes later, I shut the service door behind me and turned to face the biting wind and driving snow, with the collar of my greatcoat pulled up around my ears and my cap jammed down over my eyebrows.

Who could be roaming at this time of night and in such weather, except that accursed spirit?

I navigated blind, straight towards the north. Was there any chance I could catch it? Probably none, given the snowflakes driving into my eyes, limiting my vision to only a few yards. My only hope was that it must be going towards the lake. Didn't they always say that criminals returned to the scene of the crime?

After ten exhausting minutes, almost out of breath and with my face frozen, I started asking myself why I had embarked on such a dangerous and potentially futile hunt. Even if I managed to find the creature, what exactly was I planning to do? Up to now, anyone coming close to it had lost his life: the young butcher who had tracked it to this point last year was no weakling and had not travelled empty-handed. And there were others. Why was I here? Was I trying to beat Owen at his own game? Was I hoping to bring back the Lord of Misrule, tied hand and foot, before the arrest he was planning for tomorrow?

The wind had reached a climax and I was beginning to feel completely lost, when I saw the hill which overlooked the lake.

I reached the brow with my lungs on fire. The visibility was much worse than on the previous night, but then came a lull in the wind and I was able to make out the near bank.

I caught my breath.

The figure was there, next to the barge, clad in a long cloak and wearing a hat. It had its back turned slightly towards me, seemingly deep in concentration about the spot where Piggott had met his end less than twenty-four hours ago.

Should I take to my heels? Should I swoop down? Should I approach furtively?

Instinct triumphed over reason. I moved towards it very slowly, descending the slope one step at a time.

Was I unaware of the danger? Certainly not, and my body tried to rebel. But I was drawn inexorably forward by a mysterious force emanating from that evil figure, and I was getting closer by the minute.

I was about twenty yards away when it turned towards me.

I stopped dead in my tracks.

The face under the hat was featureless. I was paralyzed with fright, but it seemed as though the figure was in shock as well.

Was I about to meet my end? What kind of creature was I facing?

The wind started again with increased ferocity, blowing a curtain of snow between it and me.

I was motionless. Petrified.

When the white curtain fell, after what seemed like an eternity but was probably no more than a few seconds, the figure had disappeared.

Or, more accurately, it was no longer in the same place. It was thirty yards out on the lake, and moving slowly forward.

My first instinct was to follow, but I remembered what the police sergeant had told me: the ice broke easily once one was away from the bank. So, without really knowing why, I started to shout at the top of my voice, commanding the creature to halt immediately. Given where it was standing, it was a miracle it hadn't drowned already.

The reaction was immediate. It froze and turned hesitantly.

'Come back to the bank!' I shouted. 'The ice won't hold you. You're in great danger.'

The figure reacted suddenly and threw itself towards me. I heard a sinister cracking sound. I closed my eyes and reopened them to see it spread-eagled on the ice, which had yielded just behind it. It got to its feet and tried to throw itself forward a second time, but slipped on the ice. Once again, a sinister cracking sound. Once again, luck was with the creature.

'Stay where you are. Don't move.'

I had wasted my breath. The figure tried a third time with the same result, yet persisted obstinately. It had to be panic which prompted such stupid behaviour. I was bewildered: panic had had no place in its cold-blooded decisions up to now. Nevertheless, it managed to stagger on to the closest bank, where it fell exhausted in to the snow.

It didn't make any sense. Already, its lack of reaction on sighting me had been very strange;
the panic after sighting me even more so. And now it was lying there inert, out of action.

I moved towards it, every nerve in my body alert, ready to react to the first sign of trouble. I stopped a few yards from it... him... her.

It was almost too good to be true.

The Lord of Misrule was lying helpless in the snow, one foot in the reeds, one hand clutching its mask. A cardboard mask, roughly fashioned, from behind which *several locks of black hair had tumbled.*

A dreadful premonition seized me.

I leapt forward and ripped off that horrible mask, only to reveal the face of... Sibyl.

19

THE FEET DO THE TALKING

'You did very well. It was far better that she not know,' observed Owen, putting down a teacup drained to the last drop. 'Yes, very well. I couldn't have wished for a better assistant for this investigation.'

It was early the following morning and I had just finished giving my friend a detailed account
of my nocturnal pursuit. I had found him taking breakfast at the inn and had been only too happy to accept his invitation to join him, my appetite having been whetted by the fresh air and my exertions.

'Now I want to know what all of this means, for I refuse to believe that young woman is a criminal.'

'Speaking of criminals,' replied Owen, consulting his fob watch, 'I would say his minutes of freedom are numbered.'

'So it's not Sibyl is it?'

Owen looked at me with commiseration:

'I told you already that you had behaved wisely.'

I looked at him in silence for a while before I asked:

'So Harry Nichols isn't dead and has started to talk?'

'The last I heard, he was still alive but unable to say a word for the time being. He'd lost a lot of blood. I got a special delivery from Wedekind just before you got here. He should be here soon.'

'And we're going to the Mansfield's – to do what?'

'To make an arrest, of course.'

'Who is it, Owen? Tell me.'

'You mean you haven't worked it out?'

'Well, not exactly.'

'You disappoint me, Achilles; I pointed you in the right direction yesterday evening. Anyway, you'll see soon enough.'

'You seem very sure of yourself. Have you any proof?'

Owen took his time finishing his toast, then replied:

'Not a shred. But I know the whole story and I know he's at bay, confused, and very frightened. And, having been left to stew overnight, not knowing whether his last victim has recovered enough to speak, he's in very poor shape. He hasn't a chance. As for your Sibyl –.'

'*My* Sibyl?' said I, in a voice trembling with emotion.

'Achilles, please. You're madly in love with her, why deny it? Having said that, I must tell you she's at the heart of this whole affair. Both directly and indirectly... Here we are, the inspector's arrived.'

Smiling at the inspector, who was already at the door, he said under his breath:

'Not a word about last night. Your actions don't concern the police.'

An hour later, in the Mansfield drawing room, where a heavy silence reigned, the grim faces of the policemen who had accompanied Wedekind did nothing to lighten the gloom. The inspector himself went from one to another of those assembled, who sat speechless and visibly ill at ease. Wedekind was followed closely by Owen, whose interest seemed to lie not in their faces but their feet.

It was a spectacle which appealed to Daphne's curiosity and she grinned with delight. Owen had invented an amusing game for her benefit. As for the others: Mansfield, Forbes, Morganstone, Mary, Nicholas, Miss Piggott and Sibyl, it was above all else fear which could be read on their faces.

Sibyl turned her dreamy eyes on me, without seeing me. Was she reliving, as I was, the strange events of the past night?

... Her breathing became stronger and her lips quivered as she gradually recovered consciousness. I held her in my arms, her head nestled in the crook of my elbow. Her magnificent black hair, sprinkled with snowflakes, streamed out as I walked.

A little earlier, I had hidden her mask and hat under my greatcoat, along with the string of tiny bells I had torn from her coat.

Why had I done that? I didn't really know myself. But there was no doubt about it, I had caught her during one of her fits of somnambulism – stopped dead by my shouts. Which had undoubtedly saved her life, for she had been heading towards the centre of the lake.

What significance should be attached to this fit of somnambulism, during which she had disguised herself as the Lord of Misrule? I wasn't very well up on such matters, but I seemed to remember that during such periods the sufferer lived in a sort of dream. In other words, one could say Sibyl was "dreaming" of being the Lord of Misrule. Which didn't really help much. What was certain was that, while already in a trance, she must have prepared her disguise in the "Ladies' Workshop," which is where I had surprised her the night of my arrival.

Could she have killed people while in a trance? I didn't think so, and the more I thought about it, the less likely I found it. In any case, I was sure I'd done the right thing in hiding the things that could remind her of the Lord of Misrule, so she wouldn't see them as she became herself again. An instinctive gesture for which Owen had congratulated me, as I pointed out earlier.

'What happened? Oh, Achilles, what are you doing? Where are we?'

'In the snow by the lake, as you can see.'

'My God! I understand. I've had another fit.'

She looked around, stunned, then asked:

'I walked out here? In this weather? That's unbelievable. And you followed me?'

'I also did something that all the textbooks advise against: I woke you up by shouting at you while you were "asleep." But you were over there.'

I indicated the farthest point she had reached on the lake and described the panic that had seized her when she heard me, despite which she had nevertheless managed to reach safe ground.

'I owe you my life, Achilles. Without you I would certainly be dead by now.'

That was by no means certain. She had only moved away from the bank once she had noticed me. There was nothing to suggest she would have done so if I hadn't been there. I refrained from pointing that out, however. I won't say anything here of the moments which followed he last remark, but it's not for want of thinking about them, for they count among the most cherished and unforgettable of my memories.

It was only when we had started retracing our tracks that she asked about the clothes:

'Why the devil was I wearing that old coat? It's bizarre. And why wasn't I wearing anything on my head? And, look, your cap is covered with snow whereas my hair has only a few flakes in it.'

'The wind must have blown the snow from your hair.'

The wind, the snow and Sibyl's beautiful hair are the memories I guard, and shall always guard, of that night. That was what I was thinking when a sharp cry of pain brought me quickly to my senses.

It was Edgar Forbes. Owen had just stopped in front of him and deliberately stepped on the tip of his foot, to the general surprise.

'It's quite painful, isn't it, Mr. Forbes?'

'You're mad, I must say,' he groaned.

'Would you be good enough to show us your feet?'

'I beg your pardon?'

'One should be enough. Yes, please remove one of your boots.'

115

'Take off one – it's out of the question.'

His face completely expressionless, Owen stared at Forbes who was having great difficulty containing himself.

'So,' continued the detective, 'you don't want to show us your feet. So be it. But you soon won't know which one to dance on. Am I making myself clear, Mr. Forbes? No? Not yet? Well let me explain to everyone. Not being able to find boots to fit him, the gentleman did the best he could: he helped himself to a pair two sizes too small for him. Because, you see, the gentleman's feet are rather large.'

Owen turned to face the astonished listeners.

'Ladies and gentlemen – or, rather, gentlemen – which amongst you is the owner of the boots Mr. Forbes is now wearing? I note they've been recently polished, perhaps to hide a lighter colour? Mr. Mansfield, please be good enough to come closer; I think they may well belong to you.'

The master of the house stepped forward and looked at Forbes from head... to toe.

'I can't be absolutely sure,' he stammered in embarrassment, 'but they do look like a pair I own, although mine are slightly lighter.'

'Thank you,' said Owen Burns, dryly.

Forbes, motionless, seemed on the verge of a breakdown.

'He's spoken, hasn't he?' he murmured.

Owen pretended not to have heard and addressed himself to Charles Mansfield again:

'Believe me, it's only a loan. Mr. Forbes isn't a thief... he's much worse than that. If he borrowed these boots without your permission and coated them several times with polish in order to change their appearance, it was purely so that you wouldn't know anything.'

Owen stopped pensively, then pulled a face:

'The problem is that walking in shoes that are too small for you is no easy matter. It's alright for a while but, little by little, it becomes intolerable: a veritable nightmare. The smallest step causes nagging pain which can be seen on your face; not to mention the way you walk, of course, which becomes quite noticeable. Yesterday evening, I found Mr. Forbes' walk very intriguing. I'm sure that if he were to show us his toes we would find signs of his martyrdom. Well, as I was saying, Mr. Forbes wanted to conceal the "loan" of the boots. Having planned to stay only a few days here, he obviously wouldn't have packed a spare pair. At the very most he would have brought a heavy-duty pair for walking in the snow, but to have worn them in the house would have attracted attention, which he wanted to avoid at all costs as I just said. The question is why that? Or why didn't he want to wear his own boots?

Owen was silent for a moment, in order to give more weight to what was about to follow. Then, looking Forbes straight in the eye he said:

'The man who stabbed Harry Nichols yesterday evening left a clear set of prints in the snow. I'm willing to bet almost anything that they were made by the pair of boots you normally wear. By the way, where are they?'

20

OWEN EXPLAINS

Defeated, Edgar Forbes offered no resistance and made a complete confession. He confessed to the attempted murder of Harry Nichols, as well as the development of a Machiavellian plot hatched against Samuel Piggott. I say "development" because his plan had, in fact failed: Piggott had not died in the manner conceived by Forbes' crafty spirit.

Harry Nichols made a rapid recovery. Needless to say, he had recognised his assailant and his testimony would have been sufficient to expose Forbes. But let me leave it to Owen Burns to explain, as he did several days after Forbes' arrest, to a select circle consisting of Mansfield, Morganstone, Wedekind and myself who were invited to appreciate "the subtleness of his reasoning which had set him rapidly on the path to truth."

'We now know the content of Piggott's testimony,' he began, playing with his cigar as if he derived pleasure from delaying the moment of lighting up. 'Everything goes back to Miss Catherine, as we expected, one of the most eligible maidens on the market. And, I would add, easy prey for any fortune hunter. The moment my friend Achilles confided to me that Miss Piggott and Edgar Forbes "had become fond of each other" in such a short period of time and without anyone else being aware, I became suspicious of Piggott's right hand man. Marriage to Miss Catherine, coupled with his competence and his position would make him a very powerful man: motive enough for a serious crime. What's more, he seemed to be determined, intelligent and level-headed; in short he fit the profile of the perfect criminal, the sort that acts cautiously and conceals its hand so as not to take the slightest risk. For him, Piggott's elimination simply boiled down to this: how to remove him without attracting the slightest suspicion and while having as watertight an alibi as possible? For it was to be feared that, if the recent murder of Piggott were not solved rapidly, his marriage to the rich heiress would attract suspicion.

'With that in mind, one only needs to examine the evidence to see just how Forbes' plan leaps out at one. Let me begin with the séances round the table, which had always left me sceptical, particularly since the spirit only used simple knocks which anyone at the table could have made, I'm sure you would agree, Mr. Morganstone?'

The medium smiled disdainfully:

'You seem to be forgetting the shaking during the last séance. If you'd been present, you would –.'

'Precisely,' said Owen. '*Those* were not made by Mr. Forbes. In fact he was the one most surprised by the astonishing change in the manifestation of the "spirit." You'll understand soon enough. Let us start with the first messages which, after the usual preliminaries to establish the credibility of the operation, proposed that Piggott, if he wanted to know the truth about Edwin's murder, should go alone to a place which would be chosen later. Do you understand: *a rendezvous without witnesses!* That smells to high heaven like a trap.

'And there's something else: *there he will learn the truth about Edwin's death.* That's very clever. For even if *he*, Piggott, senses danger it will be very difficult for him, in the Mansfield's eyes, to refuse to go. What would his fiancé think of a coward who passes up the opportunity to shed light on an event which has hung so heavily over the family?

'Now we can see the murderer's plan quite clearly: lure his intended victim to an isolated spot of his choice, there to dispose of him at leisure. Will he kill Piggott by his own hand or will he use an accomplice? Let's look at what other information we have. For some time, several witnesses – including myself – have heard Harry Nichols speak of Piggott in insulting terms, even going so far as to threaten him. We know more or less the reason for the bitterness: Piggott had arranged for the young Nichols to be sent away from his loved-one, with the help of a personal friend of Piggott, employer of the latter. I actually had occasion to meet Nichols in the pub shortly before the tragedy. He was with Forbes, who beat a retreat as soon as he saw me, and in a furtive manner which intrigued me considerably. Forbes, right-hand man of Piggott, meeting with the ex-fiancé of Miss Sibyl! Surprising, to say the least. And what, for that matter, could they be talking about? Who better placed than Forbes to tell Nichols about the disloyal dealings of his employer?

The scene is fairly easy to imagine and Forbes probably didn't have to strain himself to describe his employer's odious conduct and probably throw in a few other anecdotes to discredit him further. And to toss out a few innocent remarks of the sort: "Ah, if only there were someone brave enough to take care of this scoundrel once and for all" to his companion – by that time foaming at the mouth with rage. In short, a few well-chosen words, plus the promise of a tidy sum, would see our impetuous Harry ready to render a service to the kingdom by ridding it of one of its vilest subjects. "I can arrange for him to be at such-and-such a place at such-and-such a date and such-and-such a time, with no witnesses," Forbes would have said, ordering another round of drinks. "The rest is up to you."

'My God, I'm beginning to see,' murmured Mansfield in a tired voice. 'He incited that excitable fellow to commit a crime. It's quite simply diabolical.'

'A perfect crime,' added Wedekind slyly, 'which put him completely in the clear. Particularly since it would happen at a time and a place perfect for covering it up. A new victim at Christmas, by the lake: it would inevitably be assumed to be the work of the Lord of Misrule.'

'We know this from his own confession,' continued Owen. 'He had been preparing to eliminate his employer for some time and was going to take advantage of the Christmas season to get the job done. When he learned that Piggott had arranged for Mr. Morganstone's services, a plan started to form, but it was only after a chance encounter with Harry in the first few days of his stay that he got the idea of a "human instrument," so to speak.'

'The one I pity the most,' sighed Charles Mansfield, 'is poor Miss Piggott.'

'Bear in mind that it could have been worse. She was within a hair's breadth of marrying that bounder,' observed Owen. 'This painful experience could be beneficial after all, because managing the estate left by her brother is not going to be easy. But let's get back to our scheming crook and the little grain of sand that pretty well threw his perfect plan into disarray. Let's go back to the last séance, the one which established the rendezvous, and where the "spirit" behaved in a totally different manner than before.'

'And what explanation do you have for that phenomenon?' asked Morganstone, coldly.

Owen kept quiet for a few seconds, then said solemnly:

'I don't have one, Mr. Morganstone. I think that probably a "force," an unknown power, intervened to put an end to Forbes' clowning. Its brutal manner is evidence of its anger.'

'Glad to hear you say that, sir,' replied the medium, with a look of appreciation in his eye.

'Now,' continued Owen, 'let's put ourselves in Forbes' shoes. So far, his plan has worked perfectly. He's ready to make the table "talk" by kicking it with his foot, so as to give Piggott his final instructions: a Piggott to whom he had already given the time of the rendezvous – the day after next, as he confessed to us. Then, suddenly, the table shudders violently and someone else takes over! And note that the message isn't to solve the enigma of Edwin's death but to *tell the truth* to Piggott, *the whole truth!* Can you imagine the terror that gripped our sorcerer's apprentice: he's in the presence of a totally inexplicable phenomenon, at least on a rational basis, and can only be explained otherwise by the intervention of a real spirit, who has come to tell the truth to Piggott, that is to say in all probability to denounce him, Forbes, and his Machiavellian plan! He's in a complete panic all the more so because the rendezvous is now! And that's when he decided to follow his employer in the hope of getting rid of him before he can "hear the voice of the spirit."

'But what actually happened, then?' asked Mansfield. 'Because, as far as I know, he didn't go as far as the lake to meet him.'

'No, his tracks in the snow prove that. So what could have happened? Why did he turn tail so close to his goal, and how did Piggott die?'

Owen waited a short while, thoughtfully, then shrugged his shoulders:

'I don't know whether it was a divine voice or simple common sense which told Piggott the "truth": that his right hand man; the man in whom he had placed so much hope; the man to whom he had extended the hand of friendship; the man in whom he confided; this man was planning to kill him and right now. Maybe he saw him at a distance, as he himself was approaching the edge of the lake, coming towards him to complete his sinister project. He was sick to his heart and, overcome by what they call in judicial circles a "moment of passing madness" –.'

'He committed suicide?' suggested Morganstone.

'That seems to be the only possible explanation,' replied Owen, nodding slowly in approval. 'The fact he had brought the dagger with him was not all that amazing given the circumstances, because he was very suspicious of the rendezvous, but I honestly think that it was only when he arrived at the lake that he thought about using it on himself.'

Mansfield and Morganstone nodded in silence, and the medium asked:

'So why, then, did Forbes turn back suddenly? And what was the shadow he saw gliding over the snow?'

'Your second question explains the first, for it was that vision that frightened him to the point of turning back and bolting like a rabbit. The reaction is simple to explain: panic, fright, maybe a degree of remorse, not forgetting the place and the terrible legend, all that was enough to suggest to his confused soul the sinister silhouette of the Lord of Misrule.

'What must have passed through his troubled mind the next day when he learnt of the death of his employer? A death which looked like murder, but a murder which no human being could have committed! And what was his accomplice going to think when he heard the news? Probably that the crime was his, Forbes', mysterious as it might appear. And it couldn't be ruled out that, sooner or later, the boy would try to blackmail him to try and make ends meet. The boy, who was under suspicion already, and whom the police were getting ready to interview. And, because it wasn't actually Harry Nichols who had committed the murder, it couldn't be ruled out that he might talk. He had to be eliminated as quickly as possible. Which is what he did, or tried to do, a very short time after we had questioned him in this same room. But, in his haste, he had left behind him some very clear prints in the snow. A mistake which he had realized a little later and which had led him to "borrow" the boots, which had, nevertheless, not prevented him from getting caught.'

21

SEEK TROUBLE AND YE SHALL FIND IT

'You're looking very sad, my friend.' Owen, still attacking his breakfast, had not bothered to look at me while addressing me. He seemed lost in the contemplation of the window sparkling in the sunshine of a beautiful June morning.

'What makes you say that?' I asked, surprised he had seen through me so easily, for I had tried to conceal the profound distress caused by some recent news.

'Oh, all sorts of things. For a start, you didn't show your habitual verve during last night's reception. But what is it? Achilles, look: someone has been amusing themselves by setting fire to some of my papers.'

He rose and went over to the hearth, foraged around among the cinders, and pulled out two or three loose sheets, each almost destroyed, which he regarded disconsolately.

'My bills,' he explained, in a very small voice.

'Come now, don't play with me. You know perfectly well that, after a certain time of night, you always use bills to light your cigars.'

He shrugged his shoulders.

'You're quite right. It's true. But why cry over split milk? They'll write to me again, don't worry. I know of no correspondents so dogged and relentless, to the point it's almost indecent. There should be a law against people like that. What was I saying?'

'There were all sorts of thing pointing to the fact I was sad.'

Owen came over, took the newspaper that was in my hand, and unfolded it.'

'Nothing is more revealing than the way people read their morning newspaper. Normally, when they are in good spirits, they clutch it firmly at eye level so as to devour as rapidly as possible the good news those pitiful liars in Fleet Street strive to fabricate.'

My friend nodded his head solemnly, his eyes still fixed on me:

'You were holding your newspaper at a respectable distance and turning the pages listlessly. Based on my observations, I would fear the worst. No, no use protesting. It's not the first time you've used my guest room after an evening of entertainment, and not the first time I've seen you with a newspaper at breakfast. You're particularly sad this morning and very unsuccessful at hiding it.

I was silent for a moment, then I asked:

'Very well, what do you want to know? Everything, down to the last detail?'

'And why not? What are friends for, if not to be there when you're down in the dumps?'

'In any case, I don't think you'd understand.'

'So it's about a woman. The classic story'

Owen went over to the window and stood with his back towards me:

'It's about the lovely Sibyl, isn't it?'

'Yes, but how the devil did you know? Did you see the article in yesterday's newspaper?'

Owen turned round, his hands deep in his dressing-gown pockets, and shrugged his shoulders.

'Of course. Do you seriously think I could have overlooked it?'

'Owen, you're a fraud! You were making a fool out of me with your theory about reading newspapers.'

'No, the theory is still valid. How many times must I remind you one of the essential axioms of our art: if someone lies to you or deceives you on some point, it doesn't mean the rest is untrue.'

I was too weary to argue. The news of Sibyl's marriage to the vicar of a poor parish in London had depressed me enormously. Certainly, I hadn't seen her for quite a while, but my heart still stopped at the sight of her name or the thought of her graceful silhouette. And the announcement of her marriage – and not the fact that it was to a man of the cloth – could not but arouse feelings of jealousy and take me back to the time she was engaged to Piggott.

More than two years had gone by since that terrible Christmas which culminated in the arrest of Edgar Forbes. What had happened since? What had happened to the principal actors of that tragedy? Edgar Forbes didn't enjoy an enviable fate, although the court showed remarkable leniency in only sentencing him to a few years in prison, presumably due in no small measure to his spontaneous confession. A propos of which, it is important I draw the reader's attention to one point in particular which is of great importance, as will be seen later. It relates to the ruse employed to send Harry Nichols away from the village for a while. Forbes had got wind of the trick. The place to which Nichols had been sent by his employer, almost overnight, is of no consequence. The latter had done so, as was recounted previously, at the request of Piggott who had also arranged for all letters addressed to Nichols to be systematically intercepted. What we had not known at the time was that it was Edwin who was behind Piggott's request! At the time, the rich businessman was unaware of the reasons for Sibyl's step-brother asking him such a favour, for he certainly would not have complied had he known that the purpose was to clear a path for his own rival. Forbes, who had overheard one of their conversations, had only a vague recollection of Edwin's words: he pretended to be worried about his sister's future, claiming that continued exposure to a thug like Nichols could only be harmful to her and insisting he be sent away by one means or another.

In the light of this revelation, it became easier to understand Piggott's words when, during a discussion just before his death, he had confided that Edwin wasn't as virtuous as he may have appeared. He had just learned from Charles Mansfield, who had in turn been told by his daughter, that Edwin's feelings for her were not in the least fraternal, a fact which suddenly made clear the real motive for Edwin's request of three years earlier.

I hadn't followed what had become of Miss Catherine Piggott. She had left for America after having sold everything, a few months after the death of her brother. The affairs of Julius Morgan stone seemed to be prospering. The tragic outcome of the Mansfield séances had, if anything, enhanced his reputation and increased the demand for his services. The vast Mansfield residence had been sold and Nicholas and Mary, who had been highly recommended, had been retained by the new owner. Charles Mansfield now owned only one of his shops in the capital. Piggott's death had dealt a mortal blow to his finances, which were scarcely redeemed by the sale of the house, already heavily mortgaged.

As for Sibyl, I had made a point of looking after her myself. I had seen her often and I think it fair to say that, after several weeks, she was beginning to have the same feeling for me as I had for her: that of undivided love. Then, little by little, there were signs of a slight decline in our ardour which, I regret to say became more and more evident. The cause was her devotion to the Salvation Army, which she had been neglecting while we had been seeing each other so frequently. She felt guilty about the neglect and blamed me for it. Without telling me in so many words, I sensed that she disapproved of my way of life. The fact that I didn't devote all my time and all my fortune to her causes was a source of disappointment to her. She clearly felt she had been called to a higher mission which left her little time to devote to me. How could I reproach her for choosing such a worthy and laudable path? That was the worst part. It wasn't so much that she rejected me, but more that I hadn't the strength to follow her. So, with a heavy heart, I resigned myself to be a powerless spectator in the slow death of our love.

Ours was not the only love that had blossomed following that tragic Christmas. One evening, while Sibyl and I were dining in a fashionable restaurant, we were astonished to see, a few tables away from us, Owen and Daphne together in intimate discussion.

During the investigation, I had certainly noticed the lively admiration Daphne had shown for Owen and the friendly interest manifested on his part for the young girl. But it had never occurred to me that any deeper feelings could exist. They seemed to be getting on very well together, and I envied them their happiness.

To say they caused a scandal would be an exaggeration, but Owen attracted a modicum of disapproval from the London gentry who observed him exclusively in the company of Daphne for weeks on end. He was seen everywhere: at the theatre, in the salons, at art exhibitions, in Hyde Park, with the slender young redhead whose age could no more be overlooked than my friend's . eccentric attire.

At the time, because of my affair with Sibyl, I had distanced myself somewhat from Owen. And, similarly, Sibyl hardly saw her sister. So it was that Owen and I had little chance to exchange confidences regarding our respective affairs with the Mansfield sisters. Curiously enough, when we resumed our lives as nocturnal drinking partners a year later and were seldom seen one without the other, we were scarcely more forthcoming on the subject even then. My failure with Sibyl was a subject I didn't wish to discuss, even with Owen. For his part, he had seldom made any reference to either of the Mansfield sisters. The only thing he had told me about Daphne, some time ago, was that she had left to live in France.

The business of the Lord of Misrule had been likewise consigned to oblivion ; or, rather, neither of us spoke of it. After Forbes' arrest, we had discussed the matter between ourselves. I had told Owen his explanations had fallen short because the legend and the other murders had been left unexplained. His answers had left me only partially satisfied : several grey areas, including some of the most important aspects of the case, remained.

Then one day, out of the blue, Owen said :

'Tell me, Achilles, have you never asked yourself any questions about that tragic business Sibyl was mixed up in ?'

'Of course. And, I must say, in regard to that particular investigation, I was a little disappointed in you.'

Owen opened his cigarette case, extracted one, and regarded it thoughtfully.

'What exactly did I tell you ?'

'You explained that the murders which occurred in the years following the death of Peter Joke, the celebrated Lord of Misrule, were doubtless the work of a family member who had decided to take revenge on the Mansfields by playing at murderous ghosts.'

'I also told you that, on top of that, you had to add various accidents occurring during festive occasions when people have a tendency to let their hair down. If there was the slightest doubt about the cause of death, it would automatically be attributed to the vengeful hand of the Lord of Misrule. All that's very true, Achilles, so what more can be said ? The events happened too long ago.'

'With regard to the death of the distant relative of the Mansfields – the old man found by two witnesses on the side of the road to the village – you told me he had simply fallen from the horse, and in falling had panicked the beast. The fatal blows to the head had been caused by the beast's own hooves ; blows which he tried to ward off as he was engaged in the unequal and confused struggle. What one of the witnesses mistook for a fight with an invisible spirit was merely the dying man's death throes, and the dark silhouette seen disappearing rapidly across the fields was non other than the horse bolting in a frightened gallop whose distant echoes were interpreted, in the fevered imagination of a witness obsessed with the legend, as the sound of bells.'

'Exactly. The sad state in which the horse returned the next day to its stables is proof enough. And it was this tragic accident, Achilles, mark my words, which started the locals talking once again about the Lord of Misrule after more than a century of hibernation. This tragic accident which occurred, may I remind you, a year before Edwin's death.'

'About which you have told me precisely nothing.'

'True. On the other hand, I did explain how the young butcher met his death two years later, that's to say the year before we became involved. He drowned, quite simply, when the ice broke under him, just as we had thought. The blood seen around the hole was from cuts and grazes caused as he was desperately trying to grip the sharp edges of the broken ice. He fell through as he was pursuing, whip in hand, over the frozen lake, the fleeing figure of the Lord of Misrule. And that fleeing figure, much lighter than the solid butcher hot on its heels, was none other than Sibyl, who – as you were later to discover in circumstances which could well have ended just as tragically – was in the habit of dressing up, whenever a fit of somnabulism seized her, in mask, hat, and coat decorated with tiny tinkling bells, in order to go out and play the part of the Lord of Misrule.

'But *why* did she do that, Owen?' I asked irritably, annoyed as much by my own ignorance as by my friend's flippant tone. 'Why ? You've never seen fit to explain that either.'

'And you, for your part, have never tried to dig deeper for an explanation. In fact, have you ever even asked yourself the question ?'

'No, because at the time you advised me not to do so, and to clear my mind of anything to do with her fits.'

There was a long silence, during which my friend concentrated on blowing a series of perfect smoke rings, which he followed with a thoughtful stare.

'After all,' I continued, 'there are quite a few things that haven't been cleared up. What use are all your grand explanations if we never find out how Edwin was killed ? You're not going to try to convince me he killed himself, like Piggott ? By the way, you didn't really convince me of that, either.'

Owen looked me in the eye for several moments, and then announced :

'I think you're ready now to hear the truth about Edwin's death.'

'What? You mean you *know*? And why only now?'

'I think you know very well what I mean, Achilles. Sibyl is no innocent bystander in the death of Edwin, far from it. Didn't I already tell you there was an artist's hand behind the crime? Yes, indeed, the fine and delicate hands of Sibyl, which have created so many beautiful things, are the same hands which caused the death of Edwin by planting in his stomach the instruments of her art, namely her knitting needles.'

22

UNDER THE HEADING OF ART

'You smiled, I recall, when I declared that this crime came under the heading of Art. Which was all the more true when the background was the most beautiful room in the house; the room where many works of art were conceived; the room which contains the last remnants of the noble tools which made the family's prestigious reputation; the room where Art is so in evidence that it's almost palpable. Do you remember, when we crossed the threshold for the first time, the extraordinary image before our eyes which seemed to be unreal, it was so beautiful? Sibyl's graceful form as she concentrated on her embroidery, seated on that delicately sculpted chair, her long hair falling over her lovely shoulders, the highlights enhanced by the light from the hearth? Yes, I believe you remember, and better than most. But you also sensed that, behind that beautiful vision, lay something tragic, some intangible sadness.

'Don't sit there with your mouth open, Achilles, and stop looking at me as if I were a creature from a strange planet. Listen carefully to what I say before you protest. Please understand first of all that Sibyl has never confided in me and I have never asked her to. However, I'm quite convinced it's the only explanation which covers the facts and is, after all, merely the fruit of common sense and logic. It's the only theory in which all the elements fall into place, even the more unusual ones, and which explains Sibyl's strange behaviour after the tragedy. Each time she had a fit of somnambulism, she transformed herself into the Lord of Misrule. In light of this undeniable fact, I believe you can now understand why I've been quiet about the tragedy up to this point: the point where you have accepted that there's no future for the two of you.'

'I'm listening,' I murmured, my voice choked with emotion.

'Let me first say,' he started, looking askance at me, 'in order to reassure you – for I see that the wound has not entirely healed – that what happened was not murder. It was an accident: an unfortunate gesture on the part of an unhappy woman.'

He paced back and forth several times in front of the window, head down, and stopped in front of his porcelain collection.

'One of my more pre-eminent colleagues advances the following theory: in order to solve a mystery, eliminate everything impossible and what's left – however improbable – will be the right answer. There probably isn't a better example than the present. I believe you

129

still have a vivid recollection of the principal events of that tragic night, as well as the notes I gave you at the time. Do you remember the testimony of the Mansfield's governor at the time: Miss Harman, whom no-one has accused of being anything but a thoroughly trustworthy person. She claimed to have seen a hideous pale face pressed against one of the corridor windows. It belonged to an individual wearing a hat and coat who vanished immediately, only to reappear a few minutes later walking furtively and hesitantly, just before being swallowed up by the tower in front of Edwin's room. The condition of the snow, together with Miss Harman's surveillance, proved that no human being could have left the room up to the point when Edwin's body was discovered. Applying the aforementioned method, what do we have?'

'Well....'

'Quite simply that nobody came out of there during the period in question. Which means that the individual with the furtive and hesitant walk was none other than Edwin.'

'*Edwin?*'

'What's left, however improbable it may seem.'

'But if it was he, why didn't the governess recognise him when he pressed his nose to the window?'

'Excellent question, Achilles. You've put your finger on it. Let me say first of all that any face pressed against a window pane is almost always going to be unrecognisable, but there's another explanation for the pallor and the frightful appearance, as you will see. In passing, let me remind you of the role played here of the dramatic accident of the previous year which set everyone thinking once more about the return of the Lord of Misrule. It's not surprising if, on seeing a pale face at the window, poor Miss Harman thinks at once of the phantom and the sinister legend. Her nerves are already on edge and that colours her testimony: for example "pale face" becomes "white mask." But that's not all. Her state of mind also has a bearing on the extraordinary phenomenon which she describes next. It's two o'clock in the morning and she finds herself in the corridor as the result of a racket which woke her from her sleep. She "sees" Sibyl in the courtyard being "held" by an assailant whom she finds difficult to describe, and for good reason. Let me remind you that it's dead of night and she's watching the scene from behind a pane of glass which, in such a period of great cold, isn't going to be perfectly transparent. She cries out and, when she opens the window, she sees Sibyl alone. The mysterious assailant has disappeared. And there's not a mark in the snow to attest to his presence. Once again, we apply our axiom: it's impossible for someone to have attacked Sibyl at that moment, or even to have approached her. Given all that's been said: that Miss Harman was obsessed by the thought of the sinister roaming spirit and the legends associated with it; that she had just been dragged from her sleep; that her view cannot have been perfect; is it not more logical to conclude that, seeing Sibyl struggling in the courtyard, she thought – let's even say "imagined" – she saw the assailant.'

'Let's suppose that's true. Let's even say that Sibyl, for who knows what reason, was beating the air about her as if she was fighting. You seem to forget one thing, Owen, even though you yourself wrote it down in your notes: Sibyl bore the marks of a recent struggle. There were bruises on her arms and shoulders, on her face and even on her lips. And, if memory serves, Sibyl herself had the impression of having been assaulted.'

'Brilliant, Achilles. A recent struggle, bruised lips: it's all there in the notes. Let's try and sort a few things out. You'll agree there's not much doubt that Sibyl, awakened suddenly from her somnambulism by Miss Harman's loud cry, was nevertheless still in the midst of a nightmare in which she was in the clutches of an assailant whom she was desperately trying to push away.'

'Granted. But she still didn't create those bruises on her arms herself.'

'No, of course not. But you still don't understand, Achilles,' Owen sighed. 'She bears the marks of a recent struggle and she's having a nightmare. It's obvious she must be reliving the struggle, isn't it? And what does the struggle suggest to you? Bruises on the arms and shoulders and bleeding around the mouth? Don't you see it yet? And whom could she have been fighting? Remember the victim, apart from his terrible wounds, had scratches on his face. Frankly, I find it hard to believe that the murderer would amuse himself by scratching the face of his victim. It doesn't fit with the other wounds and suggests the hand of a woman trying to defend herself, rather than that of a murderous monster.'

'I see now. Edwin and Sibyl had a disagreement earlier on.'

'Exactly. And a disagreement whose nature can be surmised, given what I just said and what we know of their relationship. He certainly wanted to – shall we say – kiss her, and she tried to rebuff him. He held her forcefully by the arms, she struggled, and there was a sort of fight which resulted in bruises and other marks corresponding exactly to what's just been noted. But where did this fight take place? And when?

131

'Before answering, I want to go back to the injuries which caused Edwin's death. Two stomach wounds made by a long and very thin blade, which caused severe internal bleeding. A thorough investigation of the supposed scene of the crime showed that the murder weapon had disappeared, which proves – in the light of what we now know – that the crime didn't occur there.

Edwin had been stabbed elsewhere, and before Miss Harman saw him going into his room. Now cast your mind back to the way Miss Harman described the prowling shadow: the terrifying pale face and the hesitant walk. The face may have been distorted by the frosted panes, but it was also distorted by suffering. As was his walk. In fact, by that time he'd already received two mortal wounds to the stomach.

'I don't know much about surgery, but I've heard that that kind of internal haemorrhage is extremely painful and that death is far from immediate, sometimes taking a very long time to come. Particularly since in this case the medical examiner commented on the extreme thinness of the blade and, consequently, the extreme fineness of the tears in the tissue. At the time, the police didn't think much about it, because there seemed little doubt about the time of the crime. In fact, that was a serious error. All the foregoing leads naturally to the conclusion that the terrible fight, the chaos, the noise, were all part of a show staged by the victim himself. A show intended to make us think a master of *Disorder* had passed through. In my experience in criminal matters, such a manœuvre is usually used to protect someone, and in this case the "someone" was the person who struck the two mortal blows, that is to say Sibyl.

'You remember, I'm sure, the objects whose disappearance we noted the day after: a knitted cardigan and a greatcoat which, the last time they were seen, were in the "Ladies Workroom." I found the coat, which belonged to Nicholas, in the wardrobe in Edwin's room, along with and old hat which, apparently, had also been in the same room. It seems quite clear that it was Edwin who took them and was, in fact, wearing them when Miss Harman took him for a prowling shadow. But what happened to the cardigan? The balls of wool and the knitting needles had been found in the room from which they had disappeared, but not in their usual place. But what of the cardigan? What did it all mean?

'Cardigan, wool, needles. You must realise that, at the stage I had reached in my deductions, it was impossible not to make a connection between the pair of needles and the mortal wounds made by a weapon which had not yet been found. Besides which, all the clues pointed to the "Ladies Workroom" as being the place where the quarrel between Sibyl and the victim had erupted, while the latter was knitting.

'It seems generally agreed that Edwin went to his room at about ten o'clock. He was certainly never seen again after that time, but let me remind you that *we only have Sibyl's word for it that he left the "Ladies Workroom" then.* In fact, they both were still in that room much later. Since the "prowling shadow" was seen by Miss Harman around midnight, I believe the tragedy must have occurred just before that: let's say a quarter to twelve.

'I recognise that this reconstruction of the crime is based purely on my own deductions, but I believe that, taking into account all the various elements – including, above all, the psychological ones – what I've described is pretty close to the truth.

'Sibyl's soul is quite clearly at the heart of the whole affair. A pure soul, but one caught up in an inextricable emotional tangle. She has barely recovered from the disappearance of her fiancé, the young Harry Nichols, when the nice, sweet Mr. Piggott starts to court her, with the blessing of her father, of whose financial difficulties she is well aware. Only she can save him by sacrificing herself – like a modern Iphigenia – on the altar of filial devotion. You're well placed, Achilles, to know Sibyl always had a pronounced sense of self-sacrifice. Add to that the ardent approaches of Edwin, for whom she holds feelings she has decided she must forever repress. Or, rather, whom she loves without truly loving. Imagine how confused her emotions must have been when she found herself alone with him in that room. Furthermore, do you recall that Daphne had caught snatches of their conversation where she heard them speak of "Mr. Piggott?"

'Edwin, who had begun to recognise the danger posed by Piggott, tried everything to prove his love for her including – and this was a fatal error – a confession of what he had already done for her. Remember, he was the true instigator of the plot to send Harry away. And that, without a shadow of doubt, was the last straw.

'Try and imagine the scene. He had beseeched her, harassed her, and tried to kiss her. But it had to have been an almost silent battle, for nobody must hear anything. Edwin realised that and tried to exploit the situation. Sibyl's defences were limited. She pushed him away as best she could in a silent struggle which turned tragic when he told her of his trickery, the ultimate proof of his love. In sudden and uncontrollable disgust she pushed him one final time... with the knitting needles in her hand. Was she fully aware of what she was doing? Then, or later, after she had hastened back to her room? I don't know exactly what went through her head at the time, but she must have been in deep despair. She must have taken a light sleeping-draught to ease her anguish. As for Edwin, he, too, was desperate. And his moral hurt must have been even harder to bear than the agonising pain in his stomach. But he kept his head. First of all, he got rid of all traces of Sibyl's act. He thought about throwing everything on the fire, but quickly realised the knitting needles would not be affected by the flames and the balls of wool might easily roll out into the hearth. He carefully wiped all traces of blood off the needles with the cardigan, which he threw on the fire, and placed needles and wool in the first drawer to hand. There was obviously no question of getting back to his room via the corridor with the dark stain visible on his shirt. He donned the first coat he could find and took a hat – more to hide his distorted features than for protection against the snowflakes just starting to fall – then went out into the courtyard to get back to his room. Once there, seeing a light in what he took to be Sibyl's room, he hastened across and pressed his distorted features against the glass, hoping perhaps for some last gesture of love on her part, then realised his mistake. It was in fact Miss Harman, to whom he gave a dreadful shock. He thought it best not to go straight to his room – for she might follow him to see if all was well – so he walked to the end of the wing where he waited a while before retracing his steps to enter his room through the tower. It was then quarter past twelve. The pain in his stomach having increased noticeably, he realised his hours were numbered. But before dying, he was determined to offer one more proof of love for the woman who had been his only reason for living: he would show her that he had spent the time up to his dying breath covering up what she had done to him. That's when he got the idea of pretending it was the work of the Lord of Misrule….

'In the description of the tragedy which you've read, I'm sure you can't have missed the striking contrast between the general disorder and the fact that certain objects were left curiously undisturbed. For example, the illuminated lamps and the wardrobe. Regarding the lamps, it's easy to understand because the carefully created scene could not be allowed to be destroyed by fire. As for the wardrobe, he couldn't have afforded to scatter the contents and risk drawing attention to the borrowed greatcoat with the tell-tale stain on its inside lining, which could have exposed his deception.

'So he used his last reserves of strength, after carefully locking the door to the corridor, to scatter "proof" of a savage attack throughout the room. He worked in silence because the room next door was occupied. He went back and forth several times behind the chink in the badly drawn curtains to make Miss Harman think there were two people in the room. He carefully piled those objects most likely to make a noise on top of the bookcase, then took several gulps of whisky to give him the courage to go through with the rest of his plan. Do you recall the almost empty bottle found near his bed, showing traces of blood? When the alcohol began to take effect, he was ready to inflict ostentatious wounds on his arms and hands. What did he use? I tend to think it was the broken glass found in the hearth, with a piece of woollen cloth probably used to muffle the sound as he broke the bottle. As his last minutes approached, he opened both tower doors to create the impression of the supposed assailant's rapid flight – and there he committed another error, forgetting the message that the virgin snow would leave – then lay down, pushing the bookcase over with his foot. To conclude the sad love story – because, after all, it is one – I must stress the extraordinary power of attraction exercised by Sibyl, for it must have been very powerful indeed to get Edwin to do what he did. Not to mention her influence over Piggott. In any case, you have a fairly good idea of what I'm talking about.'

I remained silent, stunned by my friend's revelations, which had, in a short space of time, unravelled the apparently insoluble mystery and fitted every incongruous element into place.

'Regarding Sibyl's behaviour after the tragedy,' he continued, 'I believe I can explain that satisfactorily as well, although there we find ourselves on the more speculative ground of pure psychology. Having read Miss Harman's testimony – according to which she saw her in the clutches of an assailant while she was sleepwalking – and looking at the scene of the tragedy, I believe Sibyl managed to persuade herself that everything was attributable to the Lord of Misrule, and that the horrific scene of her fight with Edwin, which she had just relived in her nightmare, had never actually taken place. She must have created her own reality and it wouldn't surprise me if she sincerely believed she had seen Edwin for the last time at ten o'clock, as she claimed. Of course, certain allusions, certain evocations, certain objects will sometimes stimulate flashes of clarity. Despite her apparent fragility, and inspired by the example of the reed (1) of the fable she didn't break, and braced herself not to bend, before those fleeting flashes of perceptiveness. By dint of wishing to believe in the existence of the Lord of Misrule – who was, by the way, the best

(1) Fables of La Fontaine: The Oak and the Reed

proof of her innocence in the matter of Edwin's death – she ended up "reviving" him.'

'The sleepwalker who "lives" his (or her) dreams.'

'Precisely. I'm by no means an expert here, but you must agree such an explanation accords perfectly with the facts, particularly since it was from that moment – the death of Edwin – that reports started to come in about a vague shadow in the night near the Mansfield house, or a fleeting white mask behind the window panes; such reports showing an upsurge around Christmas time. And note also that it was Sibyl, in her normal state, who was by far the most worried by the appearance of that "creature." The intensity of her fright was proportional to her belief in the myth, and hence her innocence.'

He stopped for a moment to stare at the fine porcelain cup which he held delicately in his fingers, but his thoughts seemed elsewhere and I saw in his eyes a strange look of bitterness.

'The one thing that's for certain,' he murmured, 'is that this whole tragic story, from beginning to end, comes under the heading of coincidence.'

'You said Art, not very long ago.'

'That, too, and far more than you think.'

I frowned, then asked:

'Speaking of coincidence, do you mean the one linking the "accident" to Edgar Forbes' murder attempts?'

'And Piggott's murder.'

'Piggott's murder?'

'That's what I said. You're surely not going to tell me that you believed the knocks on the table were caused by a real spirit, are you?'

EPILOGUE

Owen had sat down in an armchair and lit a cigar while I waited, hanging on his every word.

'Yes,' he said. 'A third criminal hand, extraordinary as it may seem, but the truth nonetheless. Only real life can offer such extraordinary coincidences. The motive? What was the motive for Piggott's death? Tell me, Achilles, what emotions did that man arouse in you? Or, rather, what was it about him that revolted you the most? Wasn't it the fact that he was profiting from his financial hold over the Mansfield family to exercise a sort of blackmail, a sad variation on "The Bartered Bride?" His marriage to Sibyl struck you as the height of injustice, admit it.'

'You know very well it did.'

'Well, you weren't the only one to feel that way. There was another person, and probably more than one, in the household who, behind the façade of smiles, nurtured a similar resentment towards Piggott. A resentment which turned into hatred over the years. But this person decided to act and in the process committed one of the most audacious murders imaginable. A summit of artistic achievement, a veritable masterpiece which commands admiration. I know how the crime was committed and I'm almost certain by whom, although there's no proof.

'This "someone" had certainly worked out everything about Forbes and his criminal designs, and had waited for the right moment to pre-empt him by arranging their *own* rendezvous with Piggott. After all, Forbes was hardly likely to blow the whistle to accuse someone else of the same trickery.'

'But how did they manage to move the table like that?'

'Childishly simple. Do you remember the fine carvings on the surface of the table? Well. There was a little hole there, a tiny little hole invisible to the naked eye, but which I detected with my magnifying glass. You take a tiny screw and you bend it at a right-angle before screwing it into the wood so that the horizontal part is only barely above the surface. An operation lasting only a few seconds and which in the darkness of the room would not be noticed by any of the observers. Now, all you need to do is to place your hands flat on the table "to evoke the spirits" and arrange for the tiny horizontal shaft to be trapped inside your ring. In that way, you have a remarkably strong leverage and I can assure you, as light as that table was, there was no need for a Herculean force to move it, just a little energy. I must add that to direct the table towards you, my friend, required that "someone" be seated close to you. Someone close to you and wearing a ring...'

I sat there speechless. The horrible suspicion which had just struck me hardened into certainty the more I thought about it.

Owen smiled weakly.

'Surprising, isn't it? That's what I told myself at first. But there wasn't only that. Do you remember the white mask seen by the two sisters the night of your arrival? The next day you looked outside under their windows, but could only find tracks made by Harry Nichols, whom you had surprised the night before wandering about the premises. You know my deductive methods by now: if no other person's tracks were there, then no other person had been there. Somebody must therefore have dangled the mask from a nearby window. That could, in theory, have been you because your room, on the floor above, was just above theirs. All you needed to have done was to attach a cardboard mask to the end of a piece of string and shake it from your window. Or perhaps Sibyl herself could have attached it to the end of a stick reaching to her sister's window. And, as we already know, she was playing at being Lord of Misrule in another way.'

Owen shook his head slowly and thoughtfully.

'What was the point of this little game? Was it a sort of prelude, or a warning to Forbes? I don't know, and it's of no importance other than it was this gesture which exposed its author.'

'All right! But tell me how she killed Piggott.'

'By planting in his chest a dagger which she had stolen earlier.'

'But *how* did she manage to reach him?'

'I'll tell you, Achilles. All in good time. But before I do, I'd like you to know you're not the only one to have suffered in this affair and that I, too fully understand what it means. I saw her frequently after the tragedy; I could claim that it was so that I might confirm my suspicions, but that would be untrue, for I was already sure I knew what had happened. No, in truth it was because I wanted as a connoisseur to study, taste, and admire the effervescent personality of this most surprising criminal, and to assess her "artistic" potential. And the more we met, the more I forgot her reprehensible crime – although there's much to be said on that score, you must admit, and she did save Forbes from the gallows by getting her blow in first – the more I realised there was a rare light in her, a rare beauty. She was –.'

'Was?' I repeated, slightly embarrassed to see tears in my friend's eyes.

'Yes, *was*, for she is no longer among us. I read it in the newspaper last week. Her name was on the list of victims of a huge fire in Paris. I told you she had gone to live in France, if you remember. She....'

Owen paused, then shrugged his shoulders with a weariness mixed with bewilderment and bitterness.

'She was the one that broke it off. She eventually became tired of me because she found I lacked originality.'

I thought that was a bit much, but I held my tongue.

'An artist, a great artist. Have you never seen her at work?

'Work? What kind of work? I don't follow you Owen. But if you would only tell me how – .'

'How she was able to kill Piggott without leaving a trace and so quickly?' said Owen with a bitter laugh. 'But it's the simplest thing in the world, Achilles! Think for a minute. There's only one way to travel rapidly on ice, a way which creates a characteristic noise which you naively mistook for the sound of whistling or sawing, although you were admittedly some distance away. As for Forbes, he was too terrified by the shadow which passed before him at high speed to really make a good witness. Come now, Achilles, it was obvious that the murderer could only have reached the lake via the stream which flowed down to the house and which passed close to the stables.'

'But the police proved that the ice – .'

' – would break if one didn't tread very carefully indeed, yes. For a person of normal weight, that is. But *she*, Achilles, she was as light as a feather. And her weight was in motion, which further reduced its attraction to the ground. And by the lakeside, where she struck Piggott, the ice was sufficiently thick to allow her to slow down in order to strike the fatal blow, before picking up speed and returning by whence she had come. You dropped out of view of the lake for one minute? It didn't need any longer to get to and from the barge, starting from the reeds in the stream which also helped hide her from view. She had a lot of luck, that's true. But she must certainly have practiced beforehand. As for the virgin snow you observed all around the victim, that on the lake's surface was fine, powdery, and constantly blown about by the wind. Besides, on ice, there is generally not much hoarfrost. You might have been able to see, by the light of the moon, signs of footprints if someone had walked there. But a thin furrow obliterated bit by bit by the swirling winds? I very much doubt it. I think you understand now. You know she was very gifted in that discipline. I had the opportunity to admire her. The grace, the lightness of a sylph. You would think she never touched the ground, that she was flying. A truly great artist.'

And then I recalled Daphne's passionate love of ice skating.

25884184R00077

Made in the USA
Lexington, KY
07 September 2013